'I'm afraid [...] **tomorrow.' Ro** [...] **with relief.**

Andy nodded, a questioning look in his eyes. 'A pity. Responsibilities at home—is that it?'

'I have a lot to do tomorrow, that's all.'

Rosie was darned if she was going to tell him her life-story so soon! Perhaps it was the champagne kicking in, but quite suddenly she decided that tonight she wasn't going to be a widow or a young single mother. She was going to be her own woman for once.

Andy leaned towards her and looked at her engagingly. 'Then we just have this evening to get to know each other, don't we?'

Judy Campbell is from Cheshire. As a teenager she spent a great year at high school in Oregon, USA, as an exchange student. She has worked in a variety of jobs, including teaching young children, being a secretary and running a small family business. Her husband comes from a medical family and one of their three grown-up children is a GP. Any spare time— when she's not writing romantic fiction—is spent playing golf, especially in the Highlands of Scotland.

Recent titles by the same author:

A HUSBAND TO TRUST
JUMPING TO CONCLUSIONS
A FAMILY TO CARE FOR

TEMPTING
DR TEMPLETON

BY
JUDY CAMPBELL

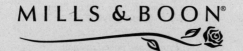

MILLS & BOON®

To George and Louis,
with lots of love.

First published in Great Britain 2002
Harlequin Mills & Boon Limited,
Eton House, 18-24 Paradise Road, Richmond, Surrey TW9 1SR

© Judy Campbell 2002

ISBN 0 263 83062 4

Set in Times Roman 10½ on 12 pt.
03-0402-49407

Printed and bound in Spain
by Litografia Rosés, S.A., Barcelona

CHAPTER ONE

ROSIE LOVEDAY clung tightly to the rope suspended down the cliff, and with a horrified shudder flicked a glance beneath her at the view. The sea glinted and sparkled in the sunshine, with small boats like butterflies skimming over the surface. Running alongside the blue curve of the water like a broad ribbon were the wide, white sands of the bay. It looked like an advertisement for some unimaginably exotic holiday resort—and mind-blowingly far away. One slip and she'd probably break every bone in her body—if not worse! She shut her eyes for a moment to block out the terrifying distance from where she was to the ground.

'Keep going, Rosie—don't just hang there!' The instructor's voice floated down to her, a cutting edge of authority in his tone. 'It's much more fun if you keep up the momentum! It's a fairly small drop.'

Rosie swallowed—small drop indeed! What she needed was an extremely large drop of something, preferably liquid and alcoholic—something that would give her a morsel of Dutch courage! She shot a look of resentment at the instructor above her. Couldn't he see she was straining every sinew to get down? Did he imagine she liked dangling in mid-air while a small crowd of onlookers watched her endeavours with interest?

She gritted her teeth with determination. He might be authoritative, but she had to concede that the man had an enthusiastic air of encouragement that made one

5

want to do one's best—and he made the activity seem interesting and fun. She'd only met him that afternoon. He'd asked to be called Andy, but the badge on his shirt read DR ANDREW TEMPLETON.

'I'm doing my best,' she squawked in a strangled voice. 'Just having a breather!'

'Well, keep it going steadily—trust me, I'm your anchor man!'

'Why on earth did I volunteer for this?' she muttered, lowering herself down a few more inches. 'I thought it was supposed to be a medical conference, not an outward bound course!'

She contemplated the crevassed rock a foot or two in front of her eyes and sighed. Of course she knew exactly why she was dangling on a fragile rope like a helpless parcel in mid-air. To impress the new practice—that was why! If they thought well of her, she might get a full partnership after a few months—and what a difference that would make to her and little Amy.

Perhaps it was worth the sheer terror of this particular moment to show how calm she could be in a crisis, how well she could 'bond' with others in a team! The practice had asked her to go to this conference on 'Basic Health in the Community' because she was young. It was assumed she'd be able to participate in the physical activities which had been thrown in as added interest to this weekend. It wasn't compulsory, but it looked better that she'd taken part, although she was beginning to wish she'd done something less testing, like swimming or country rambling. No wonder there were only two volunteers for this activity—her and another man!

Risking a quick look up at Andy, Rosie could see

his strong legs braced at the top, with the extra safety rope tied round his waist snaking down to where it was clipped to her harness.

His strong voice cut into her thoughts. 'Keep moving—you're doing really well,' he called down. 'Bob's ready to start behind you.'

'I'm going as quickly as I can!' she shouted back hoarsely.

'Just keep your legs straight and lean back—push the rocks with your feet, feeding the rope through your grip in a controlled manner. The braking device on your harness won't let you slip!'

I'll give him 'controlled manner', thought Rosie, gamely trying to do what he'd told her. Holding her breath, she gingerly lowered herself further, and with an unbelievable sense of relief she felt her feet on firm ground at last. Her knees wobbled like jelly, and her heart pounded—but she'd done it!

With a sense of exhilaration she grinned up triumphantly at Andy's tall figure at the top. Putting both hands up in the air, she yelled exultantly, 'Yes!'

She heard him give a deep chuckle. 'Well done! That was fairly easy, wasn't it? Next time we'll do the steeper one...'

'In your dreams,' murmured Rosie to herself. In her estimation she'd demonstrated just how incredibly brave she could be. She was darned if she'd push herself any further. One could push one's luck too far, and she had responsibilities, which included a two-year-old little girl, not to mention a mad dog and a slightly eccentric aunt! No, she was delighted to have achieved what she had, but now she'd been there, done that!

She watched as Bob, a burly GP from London, began

his descent behind her—he'd seemed impressively confident as they'd stood together at the top.

'I've never done anything like this before,' he'd informed Andy and herself breezily, 'but I'm a natural sportsman, so I don't think it will pose many problems. There's nothing I enjoy more than throwing myself into a challenging situation!'

'It doesn't do to be over-confident—take it reasonably easily,' Andy had warned. 'I want you to enjoy this, but be aware of your limited experience in this activity—do what I say.'

'Oh, don't be an old woman!' Bob had laughed easily. 'Something like this doesn't worry me in the least! I like to push myself a little. Shall I set off now?'

For a second Andy's eyes had locked with Rosie's in amused exasperation. Then he'd said mildly, 'Perhaps we'll let Rosie go first. With your confidence you won't mind waiting a few minutes.'

And that was why Rosie was now safely on the ground and watching Bob scramble rather awkwardly over the top, his short legs scuttling against the sides of the cliff. He paused for a while before moving, looking down towards her, then after a long time he started to descend extremely slowly, inching his way along like a cumbersome snail and taking long halts with his helmeted head pressed against the cliff wall. Rosie was surprised. One would have thought a man with his confidence would have let himself go a little more, not look as rigid and tense as he did!

'You're doing well, Bob,' called Andy encouragingly. 'Keep it going steadily.'

Bob didn't reply, but about eight feet from the ground he came to a complete halt and looked down at Rosie. His face was rather white and he was breathing rapidly.

'Think I'll jump down from here,' he muttered, and started to unclip his harness from the rope.

'Do you think that's wise?' said Rosie anxiously. 'You've only a little way to go, but it's still quite a big jump!'

'I don't like dangling on this rope thing—I want to get this over as quickly as possible. I'll be OK.'

From the top Andy's voice bellowed down, 'What the hell are you doing, man? Don't be crazy—it's too far to jump!'

'I feel trapped in this damn harness—I've got to get off this cliff now!'

There was an edge of panic in the man's voice and Rosie ran towards him, forcing her voice to be calm and firm.

'Now, Bob, you're nearly there. Just let yourself out a little at a time, and you'll be on the ground in no time.'

He didn't reply and she felt herself freeze in alarm as she watched him spring outwards from the rock and fall heavily to the sand below. He gave a gasp of agony and curled up, clutching his leg. Rosie gave a quick intake of breath, and then rushed towards his prone figure, squatting down beside him.

'Keep still, Bob. Just tell me where it hurts,' she said authoritatively, sweeping her eyes assessingly over the awkward position of his legs.

Bob's face was twisted in pain, his complexion grey. 'I've done something pretty serious, I think,' he grunted. 'I felt it go as I landed—probably my left tibia. I did everything right—relaxed my ankles and knees to let them take the stress.' He gave a little groan. 'Normally I'm very light on my feet,' he whispered.

Not light enough, thought Rosie grimly, looking round about her. The crowds on the sands seemed to have melted away and the beach looked deserted. She pulled off the thin sweater she was wearing over her T-shirt and laid it over the man's shoulders to keep in his body heat. She started to feel delicately round the top of his boot but didn't undo the laces.

She flicked her glance up to watch Andy's athletic figure, which seemed to float down the hill in a matter of seconds. He sprinted towards them, pulling off his safety helmet and revealing a thick crop of russet hair over a pair of rather startling blue eyes.

'At a guess, I'd say Bob's fractured his fib and tib,' she murmured to Andy as he knelt beside her. 'I won't touch his boot—I don't want to risk any arterial damage from broken bones. I think it's better to try and keep it stable and let them cut off the boot in hospital— he's going to have to have an X-ray. What do you think?'

'Good idea,' he replied briefly. 'And we'll keep his helmet on as well in case he's injured his spine in any way.' He pulled his mobile phone out of his shorts pocket and punched out some numbers.

'Dr Andy Templeton here,' he said tersely into the phone. 'I need an ambulance to stretcher a patient who's had an accident at the base of Lowther Cliffs, in the little inlet. Broken leg indicated—possible Pott's fracture of fibula, fracture of tibia, possible spinal injury.' He turned to Bob. 'Don't worry—they should be here in five to ten minutes, so let's try and keep you comfortable.'

He went over to a rucksack which was lying on the

sand near his abseiling equipment and pulled out a small folded rug, which he placed gently over the stricken man. He frowned at Bob's leg, awkwardly flung in front of him, and looked at Rosie.

'What do you think about using his other leg as a splint to immobilise his injury until the paramedics get here?'

Rosie bit her lip doubtfully. 'We'd have to bind it above the fracture site. We shouldn't risk disturbing the injury.'

Andy nodded. 'We'll have to be careful—I've got bandages here. I'll hold the injured leg while you bind them on the upper thighs. Poor old Bob's in shock—I don't want to put him through more pain than he's in already.'

He watched as Rosie nimbly bound the two legs together above the knee, causing as little disturbance to the broken leg as possible, and placed a pad of bandages between the man's knees.

'Well done, Doctor,' he murmured. 'Just the right touch!'

She grinned wryly at him. 'To be honest, I didn't think this was to be part of the afternoon's activity!'

A rather shamefaced look crossed Bob's white face. 'I'm sorry,' he muttered. 'I rather lost it then. I just froze somehow, and thought the only way I could get down was to jump. I didn't mean to disobey orders.'

Andy smiled reassuringly and patted Bob's hand. 'It can take people like that. People who are very athletic and used to pushing themselves sometimes react strangely when they're letting themselves down from a height. You were doing really well until then.'

Rosie flicked a quick look at Andy, appreciating his sensitivity in trying to boost Bob's low morale and embarrassment by praising him instead of telling him how darned stupid he'd been!

The ambulance wasn't long in coming and Bob was carefully stretchered away with a collar supporting his neck to keep it stable. He looked mournfully at Rosie and Andy.

'Thank you,' he whispered. 'You'll tell my wife what's happened, won't you? She's going to be furious with me—I did my Achilles tendon in only last year, playing tennis on holiday!'

'I'll come and see you at the hospital later when I've taken my gear back,' said Andy. 'Keep calm!'

He watched Bob being carried to the ambulance and added dryly, 'And I thought he was a great athlete—he never even mentioned he'd been injured last year as well!'

Rosie gave a guilty laugh. 'Poor old Bob. He seems to think he's Superman until he actually has to perform! I feel really sorry for him, though—I guess he'll be spending a long time in plaster.'

She tugged off her helmet and her thick honey-coloured hair sprang out in a disordered way around her shoulders. She ran a hand through it and sighed. 'What a shame to end the afternoon this way!'

There was something akin to admiration in Andy's eyes as he looked at her, and the firm lines of his face softened, making him look suddenly more boyish.

'You know, you did a great job there, trying to keep Bob calm and assessing his injuries. I was really grateful someone sensible was down there with him and not a member of the general public, trying to rip off his boots or giving him brandy, or some such foolish thing!'

He put his hands on her shoulders and his eyes twinkled. 'I could soon make a mountain rescuer of you. Obviously your medical skills are second to none, and you seemed to tackle the abseiling pretty well. Have you ever done any climbing before?'

She smiled wanly. 'Certainly not—wasn't it obvious? I couldn't even climb a rope in the school gym!'

He raised his eyebrows in a flattering expression of surprise. 'Great stuff, then! As you can see, occasionally people do seize up completely!'

He smiled broadly at her, white even teeth contrasting with his tanned face, laughing blue eyes holding hers just slightly too long for comfort. Quite suddenly Rosie felt a curious sense of heightened awareness— the hairs on the back of her neck started to prickle without warning, and she did a double-take. She hadn't realised, in her terror-induced state before the abseiling, that Andy Templeton was quite so amazing—he was gorgeous! It wasn't just his unusual colouring, she decided, it was his expressive face, firm mouth and lively eyes that held her—not to mention over six feet of impressive bodywork!

Somewhere within her, a sad little memory tugged, a memory of an equally dishy man, with a special smile only for her. The grief was beginning to fade now, but every so often something unexpected would happen that would trigger Tony back into focus and reinforce her acute feelings of loneliness.

She shook herself mentally. Dwelling on the past only made her sad, and didn't help Amy. Her life had turned in a completely different direction since Tony had died and her uncle had left her the cottage in Cornwall. Miraculously she'd got a job with a local GP practice as an associate partner. It was exciting and a new beginning—but still left her as a single mother bringing up a baby by herself. Everywhere she went, even on this medical conference, people seemed to be in couples. It was hard not to feel the odd one out most of the time...

Andy was regarding her wistful face with amused curiosity. 'Ready for some more?' he asked. 'I do a good line in rock-climbing!'

Rosie jerked herself back to the present and shook her head with a laugh. 'I think I've had enough excitement for today. I have to make a phone call, and I'm going to have a soak in a hot bath before the dinner this evening. I feel a complete mess—in urgent need of complete reparation!'

His eyes swept appreciatively over her tall, well-proportioned body. 'I don't think anything too radical is needed,' he murmured. 'Perhaps I'll see you later, then?' This time there was no mistaking the intimate way he looked into her eyes, and he gave a slow, devastating smile that sent an unaccustomed little shock through her body.

Rosie bit her lip wryly. It must be the relief of having finished the abseiling exercise without actually killing herself that seemed to be making her particularly susceptible to this man's undoubted attraction, as well as the competent way he had taken over when Bob had fallen. She knew that nobody ever could make her pulse race like Tony had done. She was convinced she would never meet anyone like him again, and that was why this...she searched for the right word...reaction was all the more extraordinary!

Then she gave a rueful shrug. In her experience these days, there were plenty of men who would give her the come-on, hoping for a quick fling with no strings attached, but when they found she had a two-year-old daughter, they seemed to melt into thin air. She mustn't let herself get too excited over a rather gorgeous instructor who happened to have compelling blue eyes and a winning grin!

'Well?' he prompted, looking at her with twinkling eyes. 'Will I see you?'

'Perhaps.' She smiled noncommittally and started to walk quickly towards the hotel. He started to match his stride to hers.

'I'll walk back with you,' he said pleasantly. 'Are you here on your own?'

Here we go, thought Rosie. Why don't I just put a placard round my neck saying, SINGLE MOTHER, LOOKING FOR SECURE RELATIONSHIP!

She looked steadily ahead of her. 'Yes,' she replied tersely. She wished he wasn't walking quite so close to her. His large frame seemed to dominate hers—it was a rather disturbing feeling.

Andy gazed at Rosie thoughtfully. He seemed to have touched a raw nerve there somewhere. He chuckled to himself. He liked a little bit of mystery to a woman. Coupled with the stunning looks of Rosie Loveday, it made an intriguing combination!

'And have you come far for the conference?' he persisted.

'No.' Her voice was crisp, inviting no further questions.

He took no notice of her reticence. 'Ah, so you're a Cornish girl, then? I'm surprised we haven't met before.'

Talk about determination—the man didn't give up easily! 'I'm not from this area,' she relented. 'I'm from the North of England, but I've started a new job.' She smiled at him. 'Now, if you'll excuse me, I must go to my room.'

Andy touched Rosie's arm before she swung away. 'Why don't we meet in the bar before dinner? I think you deserve a drink after that little drama this afternoon—it would be a sort of "thank you".'

Rosie hesitated for a moment. There was nothing so ghastly as turning up alone to these dinners where everyone else in the room had a partner, and one stood out as the only 'single' in the place. A drink with Andy before the meal might give her Dutch courage for the evening. In the old days, with Tony by her side, she had brimmed with social confidence, but since his death she had hated the thought of these big gatherings. Absurdly now she felt she stood out as alone and un-attached, and that was why she very rarely went to parties even when she knew many of the people there.

'That…that would be nice,' she agreed. 'I'll see you later, then.'

He watched her disappear to the lifts, her thick hair bouncing, her long legs swinging, and a little smile lifted his firm lips.

'You're a bit of a beautiful enigma, Dr Rosie Loveday,' he murmured. 'Could make for an interesting evening…'

Despite the factor 20 sunscreen Rosie had slapped on her face that afternoon, her skin had begun to resemble her name, she thought wryly. She toned it down with a hint of foundation and swept her springy hair back from her face with two combs. She looked critically at herself in the mirror—her old standby, the black crêpe trouser suit, had stood up well over two seasons, but it was about time she got herself something new.

She sighed. Tony had always loved her in black. He'd thought it looked smart, but she was just beginning to wish she had something more daring to wear—something that didn't have to co-ordinate with everything else in her wardrobe, which was mostly navy blue or black! Perhaps, she thought optimistically, she'd buy herself something wild with her first pay cheque! Then she laughed ruefully at herself. Not much point in buying something like that if you never went out anywhere... Her evenings over the past two years had been mainly concerned with coping with a baby's multifarious needs when she'd come home exhausted from work.

She picked up the photo she'd propped up on the bedside table and a tender smile curved her lips. Amy looked so adorable with her sweet round little face and springy hair so like her own. She was in the arms of Auntie Lily, who was looking after her while Rosie was at the conference. Rosie bit her lip reflectively. Lily was a darling, and happy to help Rosie as much as she could—but was it too much to expect her to look after a lively toddler for two days when she wasn't in the first flush of youth?

Rosie sighed. It was useless to worry. She'd rung Lily, who'd assured her that she and Amy were having a marvellous time making cakes, and later both of them were going to do finger-painting. She was lucky that Lily lived with them—invaluable when there was a last-minute panic if either she was unwell, or Amy was ill and couldn't go to the childminder, even though Lily still had her own fashion business.

She put down the photo and glanced at her watch. It was getting late and she would have to go and meet Andy Templeton. Rosie felt a moment's panic as she thought of the evening before her, and the fact that it had been so long since she'd actually had to be sociable. With a flutter of alarm she realised that it was the first time in nearly three years that she'd actually been to a large gathering where she knew precisely no one! What on earth would she talk to this Andy about? Her knowledge of sports was rather limited, and he probably wouldn't be interested in the life and times of her little Amy.

The hubbub of voices and chink of glasses floated over to Rosie as she stepped out of the lift. She swallowed and clutched her handbag more tightly. Come on, get a grip, she told herself sternly. This is the beginning of your new life. Surely if she could abseil down a perpendicular slope she could face a drink with an attractive man!

'Great!' said a cheerful voice in her ear. 'I'm glad you're on time—I thought perhaps a little bubbly might be a good start to the evening!'

Andy materialised before her, with two glasses of pink champagne in his hand. He looked down at her smilingly, his eyes sweeping over her tall figure and her halo of pre-Raphaelite honey-coloured hair.

'Here's to a good evening,' he murmured, taking her elbow and leading her to a seat in a small alcove.

Andy looked good—too good to be true. Rosie's heart fluttered a little as his hand touched her arm. She sensed other women in the room flicking covert looks at his tall figure, set off to advantage in his dinner jacket and his noticeable shock of tawny hair, as he strode confidently across the room. She flushed slightly—they were probably thinking that he and she were an item! Let them think it, then, she thought de-

fiantly. It had been too long since she'd had any kind
of escort, and even if it was just for one evening, she'd
make the most of it! She sat down carefully and raised
her glass to Andy.

'*Salut!* I need this after Bob's mishap, not to mention
the torture you put me through this afternoon!'

'Nonsense!' He grinned with that boyish teasing
look she was beginning to realise was part of Andy
Templeton's style. 'You loved every minute. And by
the way, I called in to see Bob after we'd parted this
afternoon, and your diagnosis was correct—tib and fib
fractures, with a badly twisted ankle, but fortunately no
spinal injuries. They're operating on him tonight, so he
may be there for a day or two.' He leaned forward and
refilled her glass. 'I hope this afternoon's little esca-
pade hasn't put you off. You know, we made quite a
good team down there—we could run our own little
emergency service between us!'

'I think I did enough of that when I was in A and E
some years ago.' She laughed.

'Well, I hope you'll be part of the country trek we're
doing tomorrow!'

Rosie smiled, almost with relief, and said quickly, 'I
can't, I'm afraid. I can only stay for the lecture tomorrow morning, then I have to get back.'

He nodded, a questioning look in his eyes. 'A pity.
Responsibilities at home—is that it?'

'I have a lot to do before Monday, that's all.'

She was darned if she was going to tell him her life
story so soon! Perhaps it was the champagne kicking
in, but quite suddenly she decided that tonight she
wasn't going to be a widow or a young single mother.
She was going to be her own woman for once—someone on the edge of a new career, independent and care-

free. It was the first time in ages that she'd had a night out on her own, and she was going to enjoy it!

Andy leaned towards her and looked at her engagingly. 'Then we just have this evening to get to know each other, don't we?'

His hand brushed against hers as he replaced the bottle, and there was a mischievous twinkle in those amazing blue eyes of his that held hers so tenaciously. Rosie nervously pulled back a tendril of hair behind her ear—it was quite ridiculous the way her heart jumped when the man looked at her! It had been so long since she'd flirted with anyone that she wasn't sure she could remember the rules of the game!

She looked at him assessingly. She couldn't believe this attractive man wasn't spoken for—there had to be a partner somewhere in his background or, if not, several gorgeous girls vying for his attention! She was intrigued to know his background—without seeming too nosy!

'So, do you instruct people in this torturous abseiling and mountain-climbing all the time?' she asked.

He chuckled. 'I know you'd get to like it if you had more training with me. But actually this is just a hobby. In the real world I'm a GP doing locum work at the moment. It suits my lifestyle as I need to have time off fairly frequently.'

'To do your mountain-climbing?'

The expression on his face changed and he frowned, a bleak look in his eyes. 'Afraid not,' he said briefly, 'There's never time. I'm always taken up with other, more pressing things when I take off. A refill of wine, Rosie?'

Rosie looked at him thoughtfully, noticing the smooth change of subject. She guessed there was a story behind that remark—but, then, who hadn't some secrets in their life they preferred to keep to themselves? She hadn't told him about Amy—why should he be interested in children and the problems of being a single parent? She smiled at him.

'I'd like to take off sometimes—I've only been abroad once, when I went to France on an exchange visit when I was thirteen. My counterpart and I hated each other on sight so it wasn't very successful!'

He laughed. 'That sounds a rather common event—perhaps it's a rite of passage in order to learn a language!'

The awkward moment had passed and Andy's cheerful demeanour reasserted itself. Rosie began to relax. Tonight was to be a light interlude in the sterner world of everyday life that she had to go back to tomorrow—at this moment she had no responsibilities except herself, and she was going to enjoy it!

The meal had finished and a man with a keyboard and a powerful voice appeared on the small stage. His songs were bouncy numbers that were easy to dance to and soon had most of the room on the floor, gyrating happily to the rhythm.

Despite Rosie's misgivings, the evening had been more fun than she could have hoped for. It was good to be looked after, asked one's opinion and, let's face it, generally flattered. Andy Templeton knew how to make a girl feel relaxed, thought Rosie with amusement. He had a blend of charm and wit that made for easy conversation, and he seemed genuinely interested in what she did. He watched the antics on the crowded dance floor for a second, then turned to her with a questioning eyebrow.

'How about giving this a try?' suggested Andy. 'What do you think?'

Rosie laughed. 'Why not?' she declared. 'I'm better at dancing than I am at abseiling!'

Perhaps it was the wine, perhaps it was because she wasn't worrying about Amy, but she felt a lightness of spirit she hadn't felt for a long time—she was glad she'd come to the conference now. She sprang from her chair and held out her hand to Andy, who took it with an amused grin and began spinning her round in time to the music. For the first time in many months Rosie felt the intoxication of enjoying herself and being alive—and with someone who seemed to enjoy life, too. She flicked a covert glance at her partner, his powerful physique with his longs legs and broad frame performing surprisingly gracefully on the crowded little dance floor. She flung herself energetically into the dance with him.

The music came to an end, and Andy swung her round one more time, his arms remaining round her so that she was held for a second against his body as it took the momentum of her spin. His eyes twinkled as they swept over her flushed face and sparkling eyes, lingering for a second on her parted lips.

'You've got great rhythm,' he murmured. 'I thought you said you were a doctor, not a dancer…'

In her heightened state, the feel of Andy's hard body against hers was almost shocking in its physicality. Was she going mad? She just wasn't 'that' sort of girl, she thought wildly, but the maleness and the strength of him in that brief second reminded her only too poignantly of what she had missed for so long.

Rosie pulled herself away from him abruptly, feeling a flush of shame that she could think these thoughts

about a total stranger. It was out of character for her
and she was probably giving out all the wrong signals.
Worse, she was letting down the memory of Tony.

It was time to go before she embarrassed herself any
more. 'I'm sorry, Andy,' she said brusquely, 'but I
must have an early night. It's been lovely, but—'

'You can't take all the excitement?' he finished for
her, with a grin. 'Perhaps one more dance? This is a
slower number, and surely you know that after vigor-
ous exercise one should wind down gently?'

It was true—the music had become slower, the
singer's voice more seductive and throbbing, and the
couples on the floor all seemed to be twined lovingly
round each other. Rosie's heart fluttered. No way was
she going to become any more intimate with Andy
Templeton. She'd had a good time—better than she
had dared to hope—but this sort of dancing with this
sort of man would be too close for comfort, and too
much of a reminder of the last time she'd been with
Tony.

She closed her eyes for a second, her last memory
of him flashing back into her mind. Tony and herself
on the dance floor, like so many of the people here.
Swaying together in a loving embrace to soft music,
his arms round her almost protectively. It had been
nearly three years ago and she had just told him she
was pregnant. Both of them had never been happier.
How could she have known that only an hour later her
happiness would be shattered?

She felt a warm hand on her shoulder and opened
her eyes. Andy was gazing down at her with a quizzically perceptive expression. 'Penny for them,' he said
lightly. 'You were a million miles away then.'

'I...I just felt a little faint,' she whispered. 'Perhaps if we went outside for a minute?'

He took her hand and led her out onto the terrace. 'Probably the heat in that place,' he said easily. 'And I imagine your cardiac rate went up a few notches during that last dance!'

It was a balmy evening, just the slightest of breezes carrying the elusive sweet smell of honeysuckle mingled with new-mown grass from the garden beyond. A silver moon hung in the sky above their heads, its luminous beam dancing on the sea beyond. Rosie took several deep breaths and smiled up at Andy apologetically.

'Sorry about that. I'm not usually such a wilting flower.'

He looked down at her seriously, his face in shadow. 'I know you're not—you're one feisty girl. You showed me that when you were abseiling this afternoon. You kept your head, doing something completely alien to you. I was impressed—not to mention the little adventure with Bob.' Andy squeezed her arm reassuringly. 'Why don't we walk down the path to the shore—get away from all that noise and heat for a minute?'

Rosie nodded. It would be a good thing to get away from those couples clasped together and reminding her too poignantly of happier times.

She felt his arm go round her shoulders as they walked down the terrace steps and there was a comfort and strength in his touch that wasn't threatening. They followed the little path round a rocky outcrop to a small private cove, completely deserted and full of moonlit shadows under the cliffs. They stopped as they reached the sea's edge and stood in silence for a moment, watching the little rills of water fluttering towards them, like frills of white lace.

'They say that every seventh wave is a big one,' he murmured absently, his foot drawing a pattern in the sand. Then he turned towards her and lifted her chin with his finger. 'Something worried you back there,' he said gently. 'What was it—a bad memory?'

A lump came to Rosie's throat. She never talked about Tony to anyone, never revealed any of the terrible loneliness and despair she'd felt at his death just as she'd become pregnant. And now, nearly three years later with a two-year-old to look after, she'd become used to that solitary state. But there was something about this evening which had triggered those feelings again. Seeing all those couples had somehow reinforced just how single she was.

She turned her head away. 'Something like that,' she murmured. She scrabbled for a tissue in her pocket and blew her nose. 'I'm OK now...don't worry. It was nothing.'

Andy turned her towards him, his voice low. 'I don't believe that. You were enjoying yourself, and suddenly that happiness disappeared. It wasn't something trivial. Why?'

She could feel those perceptive blue eyes searching her face, trying to find the truth, trying to make her reveal the reason for her unhappiness. She swallowed, amazed at the temptation she felt welling up inside her to do just that—to lay bare her feelings for the first time to someone she'd only met that afternoon!

She sighed. 'I don't think it would interest you to know about my private life.'

'You are so wrong,' he whispered softly. 'I hate to see you look so sad. A beautiful girl like you should be happy…and you are so beautiful,' he added almost inaudibly. 'Won't you tell me what's wrong?'

She looked up at him indecisively. He was so gentle and concerned. He had a companionable air about him, and perhaps it would be easier to tell Andy than to tell someone she knew very well about the memories that had been brought back that evening.

She clasped her hands together and looked out to the inky waters of the sea. 'I think it was the music that did it…' she murmured slowly. 'You see, it was very like the music that was playing the night my husband was killed—nearly three years ago now.' She halted and swallowed, trying to control her emotions. 'We…we'd had such a happy evening. It was our wedding anniversary, and…and I'd just told him some very good news. I remember thinking as we danced that I'd never been happier.'

Andy's hand took hers and squeezed it silently as she said flatly, 'An hour later he went out to get the car and was knocked down by a drunk driver. I never even had the chance to say goodbye…'

The shocking words, so baldly told, hung in the still air for a moment. She laid her head on Andy's chest and felt his arms go round her comfortingly. He didn't say anything for a long time—just rocked her backwards and forwards gently. The soothing motion calmed her mind. She even smiled to herself in the dark. There! She'd told her sad little story, and it hadn't been so hard after all. She relaxed against his broad frame and gradually began to be aware of the steady thump of his heartbeat against hers. He shifted slightly and smoothed back her hair from her eyes, then bent his head and brushed his lips across her forehead.

'Rosie,' he whispered. 'You've been carrying that

around with you for nearly three years? It's quite a long time to be lonely.'

A dart of fire ran like an electric current through Rosie's body. It had been so long since she'd been caressed, or had even wanted to be. That warm sympathy and his firm clasp sent a lick of desire through her that she'd thought she'd never feel again. It was as if after the catharsis of pouring out her personal tragedy, she needed the physical comfort she had been denied so long. Andy was a good, kind man—she'd learned that during the afternoon. She couldn't help yearning to be held by him for just a comforting moment.

She twisted against him so that they stood against each other, hip to hip, her breasts just touching his chest. In the shadows of the night, she could barely see him, but with an indescribable feeling of need her arms wound round his neck and she pulled his face to hers, so close she could smell the maleness of him, the clean, soapy smell of his hair.

'Kiss me, Andy,' she said tremulously.

Without a word his mouth came down on hers, softly at first, then more firmly. Rosie felt her insides liquefy with longing and opened her mouth to his. She felt his body harden with desire, his arms pressing her against him as she arched against his solid frame. Then he lifted her up and carried her to the soft sand in the shadows of the rocks, laying her gently down.

His hand stroked the soft peach of her cheek.

'Has there been no one else since your husband?' He said softly.

'No one,' she murmured.

'It can get very lonely, can't it?'

His voice had a sigh of longing in it—almost as if

he knew very well what it was like to be without love or companionship. Dreamily Rosie wondered if he had ever had a special person, then his body straddled hers and she was only aware of her own body's response to his. Gentle hands unbuttoned her tunic top and pulled it back, and a heady, disorientated feeling swirled around in her head. Perhaps she was crazy, but she only knew that she wanted to blank out the loneliness of the past years—and, dammit, to show that she could love again.

He propped himself up on his elbows above her. She could see his face, white in the half-light. 'You are so beautiful,' he whispered thickly. 'But you know where this is leading to, don't you? Are you sure you want me to make love to you? Tell me to stop and I will. I don't want to do anything you don't want me to do.'

Rosie stretched under him and smiled. 'Yes, yes,' she murmured breathlessly. 'Of course I want this. Don't you?'

For answer he pushed back the tendrils of hair from her forehead and bent his face close to hers, trailing his lips softly over her mouth to the little hollow in her neck. His voice was scarcely audible.

'Rosie, if you knew how much I've wanted you— how much I've longed to hold you close to me all evening…'

Then his body was heavy on hers, his hands exploring her most secret places, butterfly kisses covering her neck and breasts. In the background the sound of the surf made a steady beat to their love-making and for the first time in nearly three years Rosie Loveday forgot she was a widow.

CHAPTER TWO

ROSIE flung her suitcase into the back of the car and took a last look back at the imposing hotel set high on the cliffs. A group of people were spilling out of the entrance after the morning's lecture—probably to get a breath of fresh air before lunch. Bleakly her eyes swept over them, looking for a tall, rangy figure with russet hair. There was no sign of him.

What did you expect? said a little voice in her head. Just because Andy Templeton promised he'd meet you at breakfast... It obviously didn't mean a thing to him. You were just a pleasant interlude to him—that's all it was.

Disappointment and sadness flickered through her mind—she had hoped the evening had meant more to him than that. She recalled his impassioned words after their love-making last night—he had sounded so sincere, so genuine, his blue eyes burning into hers, his voice husky with emotion.

'My beautiful Rosie. You have such fire in you, such ardour... It was so wonderful...' His lips had brushed hers gently, intimately, his hands still holding her body in gentle possession. 'Don't you dare leave this weekend until we've made a date to see each other again. I shall be waiting for you at breakfast...promise?'

'Yes,' she'd murmured, languid after the passion of their love-making. 'Of course I'll be there.'

He'd never arrived, neither had he been at the lecture. Gloomily Rosie had to acknowledge that he had changed his mind or, more likely, forgotten completely about her—she obviously hadn't registered for very long with him! She cast one more hopeful look around, then she shrugged her shoulders and got into her car, accelerating out of the drive in a spurt of gravel.

How incredibly naïve of her to suppose that their one night of love would mean anything at all to Andy! Why kid herself that she would ever see him again? The man was probably terrified of bumping into her— being sucked into a relationship by a predatory single woman! Easy come, easy go, she thought wryly. He would regard it as a perk of the job—picking up lonely women and making love to them.

And yet, she thought sadly, he hadn't seemed that sort of man at all, rather the reverse—responsible, fun and thoughtful. She'd seen all that when he'd been teaching her how to abseil and when dealing with Bob's accident. She'd felt she'd really got to know him that afternoon, and that had been reinforced during the evening.

'Stupid fool. I was reading all the wrong signals. I had too much wine, and he was too dishy,' she muttered as she sped down the dual carriageway. 'I must have been completely mad, and madder still to allow it to mean so much to me. After all, I don't own the man!'

The most shaming thing of all was that she had loved every single, nerve-tingling moment of making love with Andy. Couldn't she still feel his hard body heavy on hers, his lips fluttering over her skin and arousing her in a way she couldn't remember having felt before? It had been wonderful, magical, and in her wildest imaginings she hadn't expected that the evening would end like that—she would never forget it.

And then there was the guilt, guilt at her pleasure when Tony's dear memory stayed with her still. How could she have enjoyed making love so much—dare she even whisper it—even more than she'd ever done with Tony? She couldn't understand it—but it was true.

'Forget about it, Rosie Loveday,' she said sternly to herself. 'Put it down to experience. You thought Andy was the kind of man who meant what he said—how wrong could you be? You've just gone and made a complete fool of yourself!'

It took barely an hour to get home, and by the time Rosie drove up to the little cottage, excitement at seeing Amy again had pushed aside some of the depressing feelings that had overtaken her earlier.

She stood for a second at the gate and looked with pleasure at the wonderful fifteenth-century 'eyebrow' cottage, with the sweeping thatch that went like brows over each upstairs window. She had never dreamed that her Uncle Bart would leave her his home when he died—with just one proviso, that his sister Lily could live with Rosie and Amy as long as she wanted. It had suited all of them perfectly. Lily had a busy life of her own but missed her brother very much. She longed to be part of her niece's life and Rosie enjoyed the security of having someone around for Amy if there was an emergency. It hadn't taken her long to decide to leave her life in the North of England and start afresh near the sea.

Rosie opened the gate and went up the path. The front door opened, and a flurry of fur and legs whirled towards her in the shape of an untidy mongrel. The plump little figure of her daughter toddled out after the dog, her face wreathed in smiles and holding her arms out for Rosie to pick her up.

Rosie swept her into her arms. 'Darling Amy—how are you, my sweet?' She buried her face into the child's soft curls and then held her away from her for a second, marvelling again at the little girl's peach-like complexion and her sweeping lashes framing big brown eyes.

Amy giggled. 'Made a cake,' she declaimed gleefully. 'For Mummy. Boggle ate some,' she added crossly.

'Then I shall eat what's left,' promised Rosie. She bent down to stroke the dog. 'You're a naughty boy, aren't you, Boggle, to eat Amy's cake?'

Lily followed Amy out of the cottage, looking as elegant as usual, even in the old jeans and pink sweater she was wearing. She kissed Rosie affectionately.

'You can go away any time you like, Rosie. Amy and I have had such fun together—haven't we, my pet? She's been so good, such a little angel!'

'She looks wonderful, Lily,' said Rosie, stroking her baby's springy hair. 'I just hope it's not tired you out— she can be quite a handful.'

Lily looked scornfully at her. 'What nonsense! If I can run my own fashion shop I can look after a two-year-old—takes more than that to knock the stuffing out of me! I'm not quite in my dotage yet, you know! Now, come in and have a cup of tea and some of this delicious cake your daughter's made for you!'

She poured out a cup of tea for them both in the little kitchen that looked over the small cottage garden with the gnarled fruit trees at the bottom, and looked enquiringly at Rosie.

'So, tell me, darling, did you enjoy the weekend— did it come up to expectations? All those lectures and outward bound activities—it's probably good to get home for a rest!'

Rosie felt her cheeks flush—she hoped that Lily couldn't see the kaleidoscope of emotions that whirled round in her brain at the moment!

'It…it was very interesting. A lot going on, but I found I wasn't very good at abseiling—don't think I'll attempt that again!'

'I should think not! It's a horribly dangerous thing— I hope the instructors were good.'

'Very good,' said Rosie hollowly, a disturbing picture of two bodies entwined on the sand dunes flashing into her mind. It was hard to believe that she had been in that extraordinary situation only a few hours before. It all seemed like a crazy dream now, the kind of thing that happened to someone else—making love under the moon on the beach with a stranger! She felt her heart give a sudden lurch at the powerful picture. It had been so wonderful, so uninhibited. She closed her eyes for a second and tried to blot out visions of Andy and the way they had made love together so passionately last night.

Aware that her aunt was looking at her curiously, Rosie gave a light little laugh. 'Yes!' she said with a bright smile, 'It was great fun—I enjoyed every minute!'

'So you reckon it was worth going—you learned something worthwhile from it?'

'Er…certainly I did. Very useful in lots of ways.' Rosie took Amy's little hairbrush from a shelf and did some concentrated brushing of the child's bright, bouncy hair. She shot a covert look at Lily, a woman of some perception. If she wasn't careful her aunt would begin to suspect there'd been more going on than lectures on community care!

She turned to Amy and nuzzled her soft little neck. 'And now, my sweet, I think we'll go and give you a bath. Mummy's brought you a little present—see, it's a little boat with two men in it!'

'A boat! A boat!' shrieked Amy joyfully. She grabbed the toy and beamed at her mother. 'Bath now!' she demanded imperiously.

Rosie watched the little girl splashing about in her bath with her myriad plastic ducks and boats and felt a glow of love for her daughter—it was so wonderful to be back with her again. There were no complications about Amy. When she was happy she smiled, when something displeased her she screamed—she wasn't ridden by feelings of guilt or shame. The world was a fascinating place where relationships were still straightforward—not like her mother, Rosie thought gloomily.

'Mummy read Amy story,' demanded Amy as she was tucked up in bed. 'Read 'bout Goldilocks!'

Rosie smiled. Amy knew the story of Goldilocks backwards, and it was always rather soothing to reread the tale for the umpteenth time—it would take her mind off the powerful mental image of Andy Templeton and her complete surrender to him.

Amy tugged impatiently at her mother's arm. 'Read, Mummy! "Once 'pon time there were three bears..."' Her voice trailed off, and Rosie laughed.

'Sorry, darling—we'll start now.'

Soon the little girl's eyes were drooping as her mother's voice lulled her to sleep with the familiar words. Rosie dropped a kiss on her daughter's flushed round cheek, then went to the window to replace the book on the sill. She stared out across the pretty garden with the field beyond and caught a glimpse of the sea between the folds of the hills. Funny, she thought, she'd never hear the sound of waves again without thinking of Andy and herself together on that moonlit shore.

You stupid fool—to him you were just a passing fancy, she said savagely to herself. You were an easy conquest, and I shouldn't think he's thought about me twice since—probably flirting with someone else now on his darn country trek. These conferences are a very good way to have a good time with a girl. No strings attached, no need to see them ever again...!

Monday morning and back to the harsh reality of work, thought Rosie grimly as she leant back in her chair, breathing deeply. Dropping Amy and Boggle off with the childminder was always an exhausting business. Amy didn't want to be left, and made her feelings quite plain, and although Rosie was sure that the little girl stopped crying when she disappeared, it left her feeling like a hard-hearted monster! She shrugged. She had no choice but to leave Amy, just like most mothers who had a job to go to, but the morning rush of getting herself and her daughter out of the house on time needed plenty of energy. Lily followed at a more leisurely pace. She had her own business, running a successful dress shop, but took her time getting there.

Rosie took a gulp of strong coffee and flicked a glance round the room. She'd only been in the job a month, but already she felt well ensconced. Everything looked just the same—a high Victorian room with an examination couch at one side, a basin with cupboards on another, and in front of the sash window with

Venetian blinds shielding them from the outside gaze a large desk with a computer on top. So mundane and ordinary, such a contrast to the giddy passions she'd experienced on Saturday night—that might have taken place in another world!

She stared thoughtfully at the blank computer screen. This might be mundane but it was security—and that was what she needed more than anything, wasn't it? Not heady nights with a gorgeous man! Coping with the death of Tony and bringing up Amy had knocked her sideways for a long time. Now things were beginning to get on an even keel—a job she enjoyed with two pleasant colleagues in Porlstone, a lovely little market town surrounded by country and not far from the sea, perfect to bring up her little girl. She looked forward to taking Amy to all the little rocky coves with their sandy beaches—they would have picnics and bathe in the sea later in the summer.

A humdrum life, she said firmly to herself as she pressed the buzzer for her first patient, was just what she needed. Stability was more important than the heady heights of a one-off affair. For Amy's sake she had to ensure that the fling she'd had with Andy was over and forgotten. She looked at her computer screen again and brought up the name of her first patient, forcing herself to concentrate on the matter in hand. After a few weeks she was a new face to most of her patients, and she was just getting to know them.

There was a brisk knock on the door and a stout, determined-looking woman and a rather sullen youth came in.

'Good morning. Do sit down, both of you,' Rosie said pleasantly, noting that the young man was limping.

'It's Chris Houseman, isn't it? And I guess you're his mum. How can I help you?'

'It's his knee, Doctor,' answered his mother for him before the young man could open his mouth. 'It's his own fault. I knew it was hurting him, but he would keep on training. I've told him over and over again to rest it and not exercise so much, but he won't take the slightest bit of notice.'

The young man made a face. 'I put an elastic bandage on it,' he muttered. 'Made no difference.'

'Perhaps I could just look at the injury,' said Rosie briskly. 'Could you pull down your jeans and lie on the couch?'

The boy glanced at his mother. 'Do I have to?' he muttered.

'Do what you're told, Chris,' snapped his mother. 'Dr Loveday's new—she's probably not used to awkward lads like you.'

'It's pure agony—I can't move it at all.'

Rosie bent over Chris's knee. It was badly swollen, red and hot to the touch.

'You've certainly done some damage there,' she remarked sympathetically. 'The knee's a complicated joint, with quite a few things that can get injured if it's twisted. And, of course, repetitive activity may cause inflammation of the tendon below the patella. It can be extremely painful.'

Chris folded his arms and said rather aggressively, 'You've got to get it better quickly. I'm in training. I'm in the inter-school league triathlon, and it could lead to county trials! I thought you could give me cortisone injections or something…I know that heals things in a jiffy!'

'We don't know precisely what the injury is yet—

and personally I wouldn't want you to have a quick fix that might mask something serious. If you started to train, thinking it felt better, it might leave you with a lifelong injury.'

'That's right, Doctor,' interjected Mrs Houseman, shooting a belligerent glance at her son. 'You tell him what to do—he might take it from you. He's a law unto himself, that one!'

Rosie went back to her seat and regarded the antagonistic mother and son. She could guess that there were stormy times in that household sometimes!

'I can't magic it better, Chris—it'll take time and treatment. Do you remember when the pain first started?'

'A few days back—while I was doing a five-mile run. It got more and more painful until I could only hobble. I've felt it a few times before, but it's always settled down. Now I couldn't run from a swarm of bees! But I've got to keep up the training, otherwise it's years of hard work down the tube—and they'll pick my brother instead of me!'

Rosie raised her eyebrows. 'You're competing against each other, then?'

'It's like ruddy warfare in our house,' remarked his mother with resignation. 'I knew if I didn't drag Chris here to see you, he wouldn't come at all. Chris and Roy may be twins, but they're always trying to be one up on each other!'

'It may be just a local inflammation of the joint lining—synovitis, or a torn ligament,' explained Rosie. 'But it could possibly be haemarthrosis—bleeding into the joint. Whatever, you're going to have to rest that knee if it's going to heal.'

'How long for?' Chris's young face looked dismayed. 'The season starts next month—I can't miss any of the competitions.'

'If you don't have it seen to, triathlons could be a distant memory!' remarked Rosie, typing some notes into her computer. 'I'm going to send you to the orthopaedic department at Porlstone General. The best way to find out what you've done is to have a tiny camera inserted in the knee that can assess the damage, and you may need to have fluid drained from it. You'll get a letter with the date of the appointment, and in the meantime I'll give you some anti-inflammatory tablets to try and reduce the swelling. Possibly the consultant may suggest physiotherapy.'

Chris shrugged. 'Yeah, yeah.' He stuck his underlip out and gazed mulishly at the ground. 'I still don't see why I can't have some cortisone injections—footballers have them.'

'I think we'll just see what kind of injury you've incurred,' said Rosie patiently. 'Remember, even if it feels better after a few days' rest, I want you to keep off it till we've got an opinion on that.'

'I'll keep him to it, Doctor,' said Mrs Houseman grimly. 'I'm sick of injuries in our house. Broken noses, arms, black eyes—we've had the lot! Casualty's my second home with my two!'

'Oh, give it a rest, Mum. Don't go on about it...'

Chris's mother raised her eyes to the ceiling. 'Kids, eh? They were such easy little things when they were young—drive me mad now!'

Rosie chuckled to herself as they went out. It was hard to imagine her little Amy being a moody teenager, but she supposed this was a taste of the future. She appreciated that the teenager was taking out his disappointment to the world in general, but it wasn't easy for his mother. Getting to know her new patients and their backgrounds was part of the interest of her job, she reflected as she finished writing up Chris's notes. Some patients were very wary of her, others were keen to meet the new doctor and a few came to her because they thought they had a fresh ear to listen to their woes!

It was a long morning's surgery—often the case on a Monday when people stored up their illnesses from the weekend. After she'd dealt with several sore throats, a child with a hacking cough and a pregnant woman with a rash, Rosie noted with relief that she'd just got one more patient—and then perhaps the reward of a lovely hot cup of coffee!

Just as she was about to buzz for the patient, the senior partner, Ben Cummings, put his head round the door.

'Nearly done and dusted?' he enquired. He came in, looking rather tired and dishevelled. 'How did the weekend go? Useful, was it?'

'Yes, rather good, although there was a lot of emphasis on deprived inner city areas. Porlstone doesn't quite fall into that category.'

'You'd be surprised. It looks quite prosperous, but there's a few pockets of real poverty around. Anyway,' he said briskly, 'sorry to interrupt, but I just wanted to let you know that we've had a bit of a hiccup. Unfortunately Roddy had an accident at the weekend—fell off that darned horse he's always galloping about on, and fractured a bone in his lumbar spine.'

Rosie looked in dismay at Ben. Roddy Turner was the other partner, full of energy and ideas.

'That's awful,' she gasped. 'It must be agonising. I take it he's in hospital?'

'Yes, he's in Porlstone General and will be for some time, I think, until they're sure the fracture's healed.'

'Poor man. I'll pop in and see him with some magazines when I can—it must be difficult for Kathy with the new baby.'

Kathy was Roddy's wife and rather isolated as they lived in the country.

'Good idea. I know he's champing at the bit to get back, but that's out of the question, of course, for a few weeks. The only good news is that Roddy's managed to find a friend he was at medical school with who can fill in here. Apparently this chap's very experienced and can come immediately—just finished a locum job in a practice near here. He's due here at lunchtime, so I'll buzz you when he comes and you can meet him.'

Ben sighed heavily. 'Poor Roddy. I am sorry for him, but selfishly I was hoping to have some time off myself and go on holiday with the family. Have to put that on the back burner now.'

Rosie looked sympathetically at him. She'd met Ben's large and boisterous family, and knew he needed a break. 'Perhaps we could see how this new man measures up,' she suggested. 'If he can cope, so can I—and you could get off for a while.'

'Perhaps,' said Ben cautiously as he went out.

Rosie bit her lip. This locum had a lot to live up to if he was to fill Roddy Turner's shoes. Roddy was such a cheery man, always willing to lend a sympathetic ear and be totally supportive, whether it was medical advice or advice on dealing with a difficult patient. As a new girl in the job, she would miss him very much. Ben, although pleasant, had a tendency to be nervous and slightly impatient—she was rather wary of going to him with a problem. It seemed that just as she was starting to feel at home in the practice, she'd have to adjust to another personality.

She sighed. That was just a selfish way of looking at the situation, and surely she'd soon get used to this new guy. She brought up the name of her next patient, Harry Rothwell, a fifty-six-year-old who would normally have seen Roddy Turner.

He was an enormous man with a ruddy complexion. He could have been suffering from myriad illnesses, thought Rosie, from heart disease to diabetes, although none showed up on his notes. There was something intimidating in the way he leaned forward in the chair, fixing her with pale blue eyes, but he sounded affable enough.

'I need some antibiotics,' he announced without preamble. 'My throat's sore.'

Patients seem very keen on prescribing for themselves, thought Rosie dryly to herself, thinking back to Chris Houseman's demands for cortisone injections!

'I'd better look at your throat first, Mr Rothwell,' she said. 'It could be viral, in which case antibiotics wouldn't help at all—they could even hinder your recovery.'

He looked at her suspiciously. 'It won't go, you know—not without antibiotics.'

He opened his mouth, however, and Rosie flashed her torch onto the back of his throat, then felt the glands at the side of his neck.

'It is rather red,' she confirmed, 'but there's no exudate or pus on the tonsils. The spread of inflamed tissue definitely has a viral look, and your glands are slightly enlarged. I'd rather you took some paracetomol and waited a few days.'

Harry Rothwell stood up and looked down at her belligerently. 'Look here—you're new, aren't you? Well, then, I'm telling you Dr Turner always gives me antibiotics when I need them. I'd rather have seen him anyway—where is he? I made my appointment with him. I don't like being fobbed off with a rookie.'

Rosie held her temper with difficulty and kept her voice even. 'He's had an accident and won't be able to see patients for a while. You said you wanted an urgent appointment and I was able to see you.' Then she added firmly, 'And I'm afraid I'm not giving you antibiotics if I don't think you need them. Come back next week if your throat is still bad—until then I suggest you gargle with antiseptic solution or salt in warm water and have plenty to drink.'

Harry Rothwell glared at her. 'This is bloody nonsense—call yourself a doctor! I might as well have asked my dog for advice! I'll tell you something for nothing. Until Dr Turner comes back I'll go to the other one—he might get me what I need!'

He gave her a final glare and stumped out of the room, slamming the door behind him. Rosie leant back in her chair and puffed out her cheeks. Was this the price of being new to the practice—people trying to bully you to get what you wanted? She shrugged. She loved the variety of the patients that general practice exposed her to, but she hoped there weren't too many like Harry Rothwell!

Rosie stood up and stretched, getting rid of the tension of the last few minutes. She wasn't going to let it worry her, although she felt a little shaky, standing up to such an unpleasant man. The thought of a strong and soothing cup of coffee was very appealing!

The buzzer sounded, and the voice of Maria Firman, one of the receptionists, came through.

'The new locum's arrived a little early—Dr Cummings asks if you'd like to go through to his room and meet him now if you're free.'

'Sure, I'll come immediately.'

Rosie stood up and smoothed down her skirt, glanced at herself in the little mirror in her drawer and went out. She passed the reception area as she went, where Maria was sorting out correspondence. She looked up at Rosie for a second and grinned at her.

'You've managed to survive the dreaded Mr Rothwell, then? He gives us receptionists hell sometimes!'

So the man had a reputation for awkwardness! Somehow it was rather comforting to feel he treated everyone the same way. 'He wasn't the easiest,' confessed Rosie.

'Never mind. You'll cheer up when you see the new locum—talk about drop-dead gorgeous,' Maria whispered. 'He's a complete knockout!'

Rosie raised her eyebrows in mock severity, and said primly, 'Is he a good doctor, though?'

Maria giggled. 'I wouldn't know that—I only know he makes *my* pulses race!'

Rosie laughed to herself as she went into Ben's room. She'd seen some of Maria's boyfriends—they weren't her idea of hunks, being built on the lines of heavyweight boxers with shaved heads and tight T-shirts that showed bulging muscles. If that was the type that made Maria's pulse race, it would make interesting viewing!

Rosie gave a quick knock and pushed the door open. Ben was standing at his desk with a man beside him—

a tall, rangy man with russet hair and very blue eyes. Quite suddenly Rosie's throat constricted so that she could hardly breathe. She stared at the man in disbelief, wondering if she was going completely mad. Was she seeing things?

'Ah,' said Ben jovially. 'Can I introduce you to our new locum? Meet Andy Templeton, our knight in shining armour come to rescue us! Andy, this is my colleague, Rosie Loveday. Perhaps we could all sit down and have some coffee and get to know each other a little better!'

There was no disguising the expression of astonishment on both their faces. Andy's eyes locked with hers in incredulity—even Ben Cummings noticed it. 'Have you two met before, then?' he said in surprise.

An amused, quizzical glint replaced the astounded look in Andy's eyes. 'We met for the first time this weekend at the conference, didn't we, Rosie?' he said lightly. 'We got to know each other rather well in one day—abseiled and coped with an accident in the afternoon, and then I had the pleasure of escorting her for a very enjoyable evening. Talk about coincidence!'

He'd enjoyed the evening so much he couldn't even be bothered to keep an appointment with me the next morning, thought Rosie wryly. Her heart began to hammer so hard she was sure both men could see it rattling her chest.

'Yes,' she said faintly, 'Talk about coincidence!'

'Well, that's great…no need for introductions, then! I'll just go and get Maria to set up some decent coffee for us.'

Ben marched out of the room and there was a second's silence, then Andy stepped towards Rosie, putting his hand on her shoulder.

'This is extraordinary,' he said in a low voice. 'I tried so hard to get in touch with you after I missed you in the morning—I didn't think our paths would cross so soon.'

An inward mirthless laugh went through Rosie. What a smoothie—she could imagine him saying that to all the women he had liaisons with...

He looked at her earnestly. 'I'm really sorry I couldn't get to meet you at breakfast-time. I felt terrible when I realised you'd gone straight after the lecture, but something cropped up...'

Rosie looked up at him coolly and stepped back from his light hold on her shoulder. 'It's quite all right—you don't need to explain, Andy. It was of no consequence...'

He looked at her keenly, his glance taking in her aloof expression. 'For God's sake, Rosie, I'd like to explain. I didn't mean to be rude—'

'Look, say no more about it—I understand completely,' she said sharply. 'We were just ships that passed in the night, weren't we? And, of course, I knew it was only a loose arrangement that we'd see each other on Sunday morning.'

An unreadable expression flitted across his face, his blue eyes holding hers for a heart-stopping, searching moment. 'Is that what you thought?' he said quietly. 'I imagined it might mean more than that to you.'

Rosie blushed. No way was she going to let him know that she'd thought of nothing but their time together since she'd last seen him, when it had meant so little to him! She wouldn't hold anything over him in any way, frighten him by assuming some long-term relationship because of their night together. She forced her voice to sound light, inconsequential.

'Look, it was a great weekend, really worthwhile. I enjoyed meeting you, and we had a lot of fun together!'

Andy nodded slowly, one eyebrow raised sardonically. 'I see. Well, I'm glad I contributed to the fun…'

There was a biting edge to his tone and the atmosphere seemed to drop several degrees. A flood of relief went over Rosie as the door flew open and Ben appeared again, bearing a large tray with coffee and biscuits.

'Right!' Ben said briskly. 'Well, apparently you two know quite a bit about each other already from the weekend, so let's fill Andy in on the practice.' He sat down and took a swift gulp of coffee. 'To be brief, we're a three-handed practice with about nine thousand patients in the Porlstone area—and we have an agency to deal with most night calls. We do have a Saturday hospital surgery that we share with other practices in the area, so we only get about one in five weeks to do.'

Andy nodded. 'That's similar to the practice I've just been at. It seems to be a good arrangement.'

Ben looked at him curiously. 'You never thought of working permanently in practice, then? I'd have thought locum work was a little disjointed—especially at your age.'

Andy shrugged. 'I have…commitments,' he said after a short pause. 'I like to be reasonably free to take off more time than I could working as a partner. If my circumstances change, then I think I'd like something more settled.'

Just what 'commitments' did he have? wondered Rosie. Perhaps he had a wife and six children, or even a business that demanded his attention. Whatever, she would probably only get to know the barest details. She would keep well away from Andy Templeton socially—from now on their relationship would be strictly professional!

She bit her lip. On reflection, it was going to be difficult to think of Andy as purely a colleague—even to be in the same room as him made her senses tingle. How could she work beside the man when every time she looked at his strong face she remembered it hovering a few inches over her own, his blue eyes holding hers, his firm mouth taking her lips, demanding, teasing and incredibly sexy?

Rosie swallowed. She had to stop thinking like this and concentrate on the matter in hand! To her intense relief, the buzzer sounded on Ben's desk. Maria's voice floated over the room.

'Sorry to interrupt, Dr Cummings. There's a call for Dr Loveday from a Mrs Joan Duthie—she's concerned about her father, Bert Lavin. Could the doctor give him a home visit? She's worried about him—he seems rather poorly.'

Rosie nodded and flicked a look at her watch. 'Tell her I'm on my way, Maria. It's nearly lunchtime so I'll go now.' She turned to the two men and said wryly, 'Wish me luck! It's not the patient I dread—it's his dogs! Mr Lavin has two huge Alsatians and they're absolutely terrifying! He's an eighty-seven-year-old with signs of heart failure—and it's hard to examine someone with two slavering dogs at your elbow!'

To her surprise, Andy stood up. 'Why don't I come along? I've time on my hands today and, although I say it myself, I've a magic touch with dogs! At the very least I could distract them while you look at the patient!'

'Great idea, Andy,' said Ben before Rosie could say

JUDY CAMPBELL

anything. 'I don't want another partner falling by the wayside!'

'I'll be fine…don't worry,' protested Rosie hastily, the thought of remaining in close proximity with Andy filling her with panic. 'They aren't really all that bad…'

'No arguing,' said Ben sternly. 'I've visited Bert in the past, and I seem to remember I thought my last hour had come! Andy can go and protect you!'

As they left the building, Rosie wondered which she was more terrified of—the dogs or the prospect of being alone with Andy Templeton!

CHAPTER THREE

'IF YOU don't mind, we'll go in my car,' suggested Andy. 'Yours looks a little snug for someone my size.'

That was true, thought Rosie, looking at his strapping frame and imagining him squeezing it into her small car. 'OK by me,' she agreed briefly, 'Bert Lavin doesn't live far away—just down the high street and third on the right—number ten.'

An unnatural silence hung between them. Neither of them said a word although they were sitting so close together. To Rosie, the embarrassment of what had happened at the weekend seemed to permeate the atmosphere like a fog. She looked at Andy's hands on the steering-wheel—strong, tanned, long-fingered. Was it only forty-eight hours ago that those same hands had been stroking her body and she had responded as if a button had been pressed on every erogenous zone she had? She shuddered. The image of the two of them locked together in a passionate embrace seemed to loom large before her on the window like the picture on a cinema screen.

'I'm glad to get the opportunity to speak to you alone, Rosie.' The sudden sound of Andy's deep voice splitting the silence was startling. 'I'd like to explain what happened on Sunday morning...'

Rosie's heart fluttered—she'd rather they laid that subject to rest!

'I've told you... it doesn't matter,' she cut in quickly.

'As I said, it was a good two days, plenty going on and very worthwhile.'

'Ah!' he murmured, a faint smile touching his lips. 'You felt you got something from the weekend, then?'

'Of course,' she faltered. 'I think I learnt a lot...' She couldn't bring herself to mention their night of love-making.

The car accelerated suddenly as he put his foot down hard on the pedal. It was as if something had snapped inside him, and he stared ahead of him, his profile stony.

'What did you learn?' he said harshly. 'To get something out of your system—obliterate the memory of your husband perhaps?'

'What?' she gasped. A white flash of anger and shame went through her. 'What on earth do you mean? How could you say something like that?'

'OK. You tell me why you wanted me to make love to you!'

'You think I was using you, do you?'

'And weren't you?' The car slowed down as it came to traffic lights. Andy turned his face towards her, his voice deliberate, cold. 'I happened to be available, a convenient male ready to fulfil your fantasies for an hour or two...'

'How dare you?' Rosie felt the nails dig into the palms of her hands with fury. 'I...I wanted to make love to you—of course I did—and you weren't entirely averse to the idea either! I...I thought that I'd met someone for the first time in many years that understood how I felt...'

Andy started the car again with a harsh jerk and shot off over the crossing. 'I thought I understood you, too,' he said bitingly. 'I hadn't realised that I was just a ship that passed in the night, as you so charmingly put it—a kind of stud to satisfy you!'

Rosie felt her face blazing with fury. What a wonderful way to start a professional relationship!

Her voice choking with emotion, she spluttered, 'Don't give me that, Andy Templeton. It was you that took the whole thing so casually. I turned up the next day to meet you—I waited outside the hotel for nearly an hour after the lecture! You never turned up. You couldn't have cared less about what we'd done!'

There was a screech of brakes as Andy turned into Mr Lavin's street and came to a skidding halt in front of his little terraced house.

'As I tried to tell you,' he rasped, turning towards her and raking her with cold blue eyes, 'something happened I couldn't ignore. I did leave a message for you—it can't have got through.'

Rosie stared at him for a minute. Did the revelation make any difference?

'So that was your excuse?' she said bitterly. To her horror, tears welled up in her eyes and she turned quickly away.

'You don't believe me?' His hand went under her chin and turned her face back to his, noting her distress. His expression suddenly became contrite, softer. 'I really did want to see you again,' he murmured, his eyes raking her face. He paused for a second, and his finger traced the line of her jaw down to the little hollow of her neck. 'I thought that the feeling was mutual. It was rather a jolt to find out from you today that our evening together had just been a pleasant interlude, had meant nothing to you at all! To me it was more than just a casual bit of fun.'

Emotions jumbled together in Rosie's head like colours in a kaleidoscope. She closed her eyes for a second—what was he telling her? That it had meant as much to him as it had to her—or now that coincidence had drawn them together, was he trying to make excuses for his non-appearance yesterday?

There was a pause, then he said quietly, 'Perhaps we should see your patient—I think I can hear the dogs barking already. We must discuss this later!'

He got out of the car briskly and came round to her side, holding the door open for her.

She followed him silently up the path and knocked on the front door. She stood away from Andy, trying to calm all the emotions that followed their conversation. He *had* sounded sorry. Perhaps he really had intended to meet her again... A cacophony of barking came from the back regions of the house, and she jumped out of her reverie. She looked apprehensively up at Andy.

'I imagine their bark's worse than their bite,' he murmured sardonically. 'Don't worry, I won't let them touch you...'

She shrugged. It was time to put personal differences to one side. If they were going to work together they were going to have to maintain a professional attitude.

'I'll quickly brief you on my patient,' she said briskly. 'Bert Lavin collapsed at a football match a few weeks ago. He was admitted to Porlstone General for a day or two with bad angina and seemed to respond well to medication. He was sent home, and I've been seeing him regularly, but he refuses to have any home help and gives the community nurse short shrift when she comes. He only seems to want his daughter.'

'Frightened of new faces and routines, I guess,' Andy observed. He sniffed as they stood by the front door as the strong aroma from a pipe drifted through the open window.

'Smells like your patient still enjoys a smoke,' he commented wryly.

'I don't think he can change the habits of a lifetime,' murmured Rosie.

They heard muffled sounds of a door being opened and a woman's voice shouting over the noise of the dogs. 'Get down, Prince! Oh, for heaven's sake, come back here, Duke!'

The door was opened a fraction, and a harassed-looking woman, still with her coat on, peered through the crack.

'I don't know what to do, Doctor. I haven't the strength to pull these darn dogs back and let you in. They aren't vicious, just very strong and they'd knock you down.'

Andy stepped in front of Rosie. 'I'm a colleague of Dr Loveday's. I'm used to dogs and quite large myself. If I go round to the back, you could let me in so that the doctor can come in here and see Mr Lavin. I'll distract the dogs and make sure they don't get through.'

Andy's voice was persuasive. Joan Duthie, Bert Lavin's daughter, looked doubtfully at him for a moment, then nodded her head.

'You go round to the back, then,' she agreed. 'They'll quieten down after a while and then you can lock them in the kitchen and come through to the front.'

'Wish me luck,' he muttered as he disappeared through the side gate. Suddenly Rosie was very grateful that he was with her!

'I'm so glad you've come, Doctor,' said Joan as she reappeared to let Rosie in from the front. 'And I'm very glad the other doctor is here to help with the dogs. I didn't want to have to send you away again. Dad seems really off. He just sits in his chair all day, and hardly eats a thing—has no energy at all. When he does get up he's so wheezy. I wish he'd come and stay with us for a while, but he won't—stubborn old man!' She sighed. 'I don't want to be selfish, but it would help me. I have to catch two buses to come across town with his shopping and to see him. It's taken nearly three hours to get here.'

'It is tough. Perhaps we can see if he can get some home help…'

Joan Duthie snorted. 'If only…' she grumbled. 'He refuses to have anyone. He's very suspicious of strangers—thinks they're after his millions!'

Rosie smiled. Like many of her elderly patients, Bert was fiercely independent and trusted only his nearest and dearest to help him.

The sound of barking dogs had gradually quietened from the back regions, and Andy joined them.

'That didn't take you long,' said Joan. 'How did you quieten them?'

Andy grinned modestly. 'They don't call me Dr Dolittle for nothing! Actually, I found two old bones in the garden and they're busy chewing on those!'

'Let me introduce Dr Templeton,' Rosie said to Joan and Bert, whose shrunken frame was ensconced in a large armchair. 'He's a colleague who's come to help me with my visits. Do you mind if he listens in?'

'He's a lucky beggar,' said Bert with a wheezy chuckle. 'Dr Loveday's a real cracker—they don't come bonnier than her. She's the best thing that's happened to that practice!'

'That's a very good description,' murmured Andy in

agreement. He glanced at Rosie and she saw his eyes dancing with laughter.

She felt her heartbeat bound into racing gear, and turned sharply away—that wasn't the kind of thing she wanted Andy Templeton to say! Rather breathlessly she said to Bert, 'I've just come to see what you're up to, Bert—find out how effective the medication is.'

He smiled a gap-toothed grin at her. 'Don't get up to anything here, gel—not much of a den of iniquity in these parts!'

Rosie laughed and lifted up Bert's thick sweater, shirt and vest so that she could put the stethoscope to his chest. She listened carefully for a moment to the 'flub-flub' of his heartbeat—it sounded rather erratic and fast.

She looked up at Andy. 'Would you have a listen, too? It would be good to have another opinion.' She dropped her voice. 'His heart's labouring a bit. Probably enlarged to try and cope with the normal volume of blood.'

After a minute he handed back her stethoscope and nodded at her. 'Sounds as if Mr Lavin could do with some vasodilator drugs—they could reduce the workload, don't you think?'

'Yes,' she agreed. 'It might help the oedema as well.' She flicked a glance at the old man's neck, noting the bulging neck veins and the swollen ankles over his old slippers. Bert had certainly deteriorated since she'd last visited him. 'I'll take some blood and do a full test for anaemia, and a urea and electrolyte test for kidney function.'

'You're nothing but a blinking vampire,' grumbled the old man, watching as she put a tourniquet on his arm and drew some blood from his vein.

Rosie put a pad of cotton wool on the puncture point and bent his arm up to hold it firm.

'Now, you're not smoking, are you, Bert?' she asked mock-sternly, neatly labelling the phials of blood she'd taken and folding her stethoscope. 'You know it's not good for your heart or your arteries.'

He looked stubbornly at her. 'Can't tell you a lie, Doc. I do have the odd pipe, but it's the only blinking pleasure I get! No women or liquor to speak of now!'

She chuckled, but looked at him with compassion. 'I'm sorry about that—but how are you feeling?'

He shrugged. 'Bloody awful—too tired to blow the top of me beer, and I've got terrible indigestion. What's causing that, do you think?'

She sat down on a little stool beside him. 'Your heart's not as efficient as it was, Bert, and that can cause a few uncomfortable problems. I'm going to write out a prescription for something that should help. I know you're on quite a few drugs at the moment, including diuretics, but there are others that could reduce the workload on your heart.'

'I can't keep up with all these blessed pills,' he grumbled. 'I'm like a flaming rattle!'

Joan sighed. 'He'll never get to grips with the different medicines he's on. I don't think he's taking the ones he's got properly—I'm sure he's getting mixed up with them all.'

'Bert,' Rosie said gently, 'is there no possibility that you'd go to your daughter's house for a few days even—just until you get used to the dosages of these drugs?'

He scowled. 'I'm not leaving here. If I do, I'll never come back! I was born here and I'll die here, so don't make me go!'

The two women looked at each other. Joan was plainly upset, seeing her father deteriorating, wanting to help, but frustrated that he wouldn't accept that help.

'If we solemnly promise that if you've improved over the next few weeks and got the hang of the medicines by then, you can come back—would you try it? Joan will get you into the routine of your medicines, and you might just consider that possibility of having a home help to take the worry off Joan's mind when you come back here.'

Rosie's voice was gentle—she knew the struggle that was going on in Bert's mind. He was frightened of the future and what would happen to him if he left all the familiar things behind.

The old man sighed and looked up for a second at the ceiling. Then he looked at his daughter, brushing tears from her eyes, and nodded very slowly. 'I don't want to be a nuisance, you know,' he growled. 'Joan's got her own life to lead, and there won't be room for an old fellow like me.'

Joan knelt by her father and put her hand on his arm. Rosie guessed that they weren't normally a very demonstrative family, but it was an emotional situation. 'Oh, Dad,' she said softly, 'you know you're never a nuisance. Come to me for a little while, please. It would be a nice rest for you, and I'd cook all your favourite things.'

'You promise I can come back?'

'Whenever you want.'

Bert leaned back in his chair and closed his eyes. 'Well…just for a while, then. And I'll be wanting to watch all the football, don't forget.' He turned sharply to Andy, watching by the doorway. 'What do you think, Doc? Should I go?'

Andy moved forward and squatted down level with the old man. 'I think you'd be very sensible to go to your daughter's and be spoiled for a while, Mr Lavin!'

Andy turned the key in the ignition and the car sprang into life. He let it idle for a few minutes.

'You did well there,' he said quietly. 'Not easy persuading someone to leave their home—even if it is for a little while.'

Rosie sighed. 'Poor Bert—he's such a plucky old soldier. I'm afraid he may not get back to his little house, even so. His heart's not good, is it?'

Andy shook his head. 'From his symptoms I'd say he's got congestive cardiac failure—the indigestion he's complaining of is probably due to back pressure in the circulation. I should think his liver's enlarged and the other symptoms are part of the knock-on effect. Perhaps in the short term, staying with his daughter will give him some more time.' Then he gave a short laugh. 'Is Joan taking those great animals with her, do you think?'

'Apparently a neighbour has been mad enough to say he'll look after them!'

Suddenly they smiled at each other. Without realising it and through discussion of a patient, the frosty atmosphere between them had risen a few degrees. Andy swung the car into the road and flicked a look across at Rosie, a slightly penitent expression on his face.

'Perhaps I was a bit harsh on you before…I'm sorry.'

'Perhaps.' Rosie's voice was neutral. She wasn't going to capitulate too much—she still felt wounded by his reference to Tony. How could she ever 'obliterate' her husband's memory? It would take more than a casual apology for her to forget that.

Andy caught the restrained note in her voice and ran a hand roughly through his hair. 'I didn't mean to hurt you—hell! I didn't mean any of it! I suppose I felt put down, my pride rather dented. To be told our evening was a mere casual fling made it all seem a little cheap…tawdry.'

'I'm sorry you thought that,' she said evenly. 'I wouldn't want to be thought cheap.'

He sighed, then said harshly, 'It wasn't cheap—of course it wasn't. It was bloody wonderful.'

With an abrupt movement he flicked the steering-wheel abruptly to the left and drew into a lay-by, stopping the car and unclicking his safety belt. Suddenly his hand was under her chin and he was lifting her face to his, holding her gaze with his burning blue eyes, so close to her that she could see the dark lashes fringing them. Rosie's heart started to bang nervously against her ribs. He was too close, far too close for comfort!

'You see, Rosie, I can't believe that you thought we were just having a casual fling—I know that you aren't that sort of girl. What we did meant more than that. There was electricity and fire between us—and something more besides.'

She felt his breath on her cheek, the clean male smell of him, and heat turned her insides to liquid as he came closer, those demanding lips tantalisingly near. Her thoughts and resolve began to dissolve far too rapidly. Every instinct in her screamed that she should twine her arms around him and start again where they'd left off the other night! Then a small but insistent voice hammered in her head, Be careful, Rosie—it would be too easy to fall for this man!

Rosie swallowed hard and twisted away from Andy slightly, furious with herself at her body's treacherous response. She mustn't—couldn't—let things get out of hand.

'Look,' she said, a hint of desperation in her voice, 'we've got to get back. I…I'm so glad we've someone to fill in for Roddy—and I'm glad it's you, Andy. But if we're going to be colleagues with a happy working relationship…well, you know as well as I do that sex and work don't mix!'

He threw back his head and laughed. 'Don't you trust me? You trusted me on Saturday night!'

It was herself she didn't trust! 'That…that was different. I didn't know then that we'd be working together. Now things have changed completely. We're colleagues—how could I concentrate on work if we…'

'Had a romance?' A slight smile quirked the side of his mouth. 'Perhaps you're right! We'll have to keep sex and work well apart, then, won't we?'

Rosie looked at him doubtfully—that wasn't quite the answer she'd expected! Did Andy agree with her or not? He swung the car onto the road again and drove back to the surgery without further comment.

As they drew up in the car park she looked at him steadily, a frown of resolve on her face. 'Perhaps we should be clear that our professional relationship starts right now!' she said briskly.

'Whatever you say, Dr Loveday—at least in working hours!'

She looked at him uncertainly for a second, then got out of the car quickly and walked towards the surgery.

Andy watched her with a wry smile. 'Perhaps she's right,' he said wryly to himself. 'But it would be difficult—darned difficult to work closely with someone like Rosie Loveday and think of nothing but work!

Slowly he got out of the car and locked the door, twisting the key savagely in the lock. Fate, he reflected angrily, might have been more kind to him. It had been a long long time since he'd felt drawn to any woman, but as soon as he'd seen Rosie's tall lissom figure and wide brown eyes he'd known it was more than an ordinary passing fancy. He was captivated by her—her looks, her manner—and he was well aware of the mutual crackle of sexual tension between them. If the phone call hadn't come when it had, he'd have met Rosie for breakfast as they'd promised each other, and not jeopardised the progress of their relationship.

He sighed. His ex-wife had a habit of throwing his life off course just when he thought it was picking up. He shouldn't be surprised—she'd done it so often before that he was beginning to think she had second sight! He walked slowly towards the surgery.

It was a quiet lunchtime. Maria was munching her sandwiches behind the glass screen of Reception and reading a health and beauty magazine with great absorption. Rosie went straight into her room and flung her briefcase onto her desk before sinking onto a chair. She could still hardly believe that the locum who was to replace Roddy Turner was the man she'd made passionate love with only two nights before! It was crazy, but it had happened, and she'd just have to make the best of it—forget that the most drop-dead gorgeous male was going to be working in the room next to hers!

She sat gazing before her rather glumly. Three days before she had been a young widow with no thoughts of romance or the future, beyond looking after Amy and working hard at her career. Suddenly everything had changed. It was almost as if Tony had given her permission to finish grieving for him that night and start life anew. And hadn't she grabbed that chance? she thought ruefully. Why had she done something so out of character as to jump into bed with the first man she met?

'Because I didn't seem able to help it,' she muttered savagely. 'I didn't expect to fall for anyone that night—but I did!'

The sudden sound of a child screaming outside in the reception area jolted Rosie back to reality. She looked up, startled, all thoughts of Andy Templeton melting away as the noise seemed to double in volume. What in heaven's name was going on? Had there been an accident? She got up and almost ran to the door, flinging it open.

Maria was standing there, a mixture of amusement and alarm on her face. A woman with a child on her knee was behind her, sitting on one of the reception area chairs. The child's screaming began to abate.

'What's happening, Maria? Has someone been hurt? It sounds as if a young child's had an accident.'

Maria shook her head. 'It's not the child that's in trouble, Rosie—it's your childminder, Veronica! She's hurt her finger. Amy's here, but she's fine—she just wants you!'

Rosie looked at her in surprise, then suddenly stiffened as a familiar little voice said loudly and demandingly, 'Want Mummy—get Mummy *now*!'

Amy's stout little figure toddled over to Rosie, her face wreathed in smiles, and flung her arms round her mother's knees in delight.

'What's happened?' asked Rosie, lifting Amy and

kissing her fat little cheek, then turning towards Veronica. 'Did you have an accident? Have you hurt yourself badly?'

Veronica's round face looked embarrassed, and rather white. 'I'm awfully sorry to bother you, Dr Loveday, but I trapped my finger in the sash window as I was trying to raise it. It's so painful, I thought I might faint, and I didn't think I could look after Rosie, feeling as I did.'

Her voice trailed off and she bit her lip, trying to keep herself from crying, then she rallied slightly. 'I hope you don't mind me coming when it's lunchtime, but you're only round the corner, and I just wondered if you could do anything about it…'

'It must be agony,' said Rosie sympathetically. 'And don't worry about coming to see us—you did the right thing. I don't want Amy's childminder collapsing! There's no one here at the moment anyway. Let me just have a quick look.'

She put Amy down on the floor again and Veronica held out her hand, palm down, revealing a nail on her swollen middle finger that was dark purple.

Rosie winced. 'Heavens—that looks nasty! I should think that's throbbing a bit!'

Veronica nodded. 'It feels really hot and tense—as if it's going to burst!'

'It's an excruciating thing to happen, but I think we can do something to get rid of the blood that's pressing against the nail—and you won't feel a thing!' she said quickly as Veronica blanched and clutched her hand protectively to her chest. 'We'll go into my room for a minute.'

Maria said helpfully, 'Shall I take Amy to have a biscuit with me while you look at the finger? Would you like that, sweetheart? Come and help me pick out the best biscuits in the barrel and perhaps a little drink of milk!'

Amy danced up and down, her blonde curls springing round her head. 'A biscuit!' She beamed. 'Lots of biscuits!'

'So this is how we keep the patients happy, is it— bribery and corruption?' An amused deep voice from the door made them all turn round. Andy was standing there, twirling his car keys in his hand. His eyes followed Amy's plump little figure, now running round the adults with her arms out like an aeroplane.

'She seems the picture of health,' he observed with a grin.

'She's not the patient,' said Rosie dryly. 'She's just here for the ride—and some biscuits—while I look at Veronica who's done something nasty to her finger. Go on with Maria, darling, and I'll be with you in a minute!'

Andy looked from Rosie to Amy and then back again, and his eyes widened in realisation. 'So that's it,' he murmured. 'It's not hard to guess whose daughter she is—same hair, same eyes, same spirit—and I didn't even know of her existence!'

Amy scampered off with Maria and he turned to Rosie and Veronica. 'Perhaps I'll be introduced to that young lady later!'

Rosie blushed. Why should she feel guilty about not mentioning to Andy that she had a child? She turned quickly to Veronica. 'Show Dr Templeton your finger, Veronica.'

Veronica held out her hand and Andy gave a low whistle. 'That's a nice subungual haematoma you've got there—pretty excruciating for you.'

'What's a subungual…what you said?' yelped
Veronica fearfully.

'You've squashed the tip of that finger and burst
some blood vessels. The blood that's collected under
your nail is a subungual haematoma. That's why it's
so painful—there isn't much room for it to expand.'
He looked at her alarmed expression and smiled.
'Don't worry—it's very sore, but it's not life-
threatening!'

'I'm going to release the pressure before the blood
clots,' said Rosie. 'I've got half of the equipment,' she
remarked. 'All I need is a match or a cigarette lighter!'

She walked into her room and, opening a drawer in
her desk, took out a pin and a pair of small tweezers.

Andy followed her. 'Let me assist with the rest of
it!'

He felt in his pocket and drew out a cigarette lighter.
'This is strictly for minor ops only—not because I
smoke,' he informed a pale-looking Veronica, who was
viewing the proceedings with distinct nervousness.

'Sit down, love,' said Rosie. 'Don't worry—this is
an easy procedure, and in a second you'll be able to
press a doorbell with that finger! Just turn round and
face the window while I hold your hand steady and Dr
Templeton deals with your nail.'

Veronica gave a little squeak of fright, but Andy
moved behind her and flicked the lighter. Rosie gave
him the pin held in the tweezers. Grasping them firmly,
he placed the tip of the pin in the lighter's flame until
it glowed red. Then he pressed the tip firmly onto the
fingernail. The slightest hiss and faint smoke appeared
as the pin burnt through the nail.

'Geronimo!' said Andy with satisfaction as he drew
the pin away. 'The blood has somewhere to go now!'

Veronica watched blood ooze through the hole in her nail with disbelief. 'Is that all you do?' she said incredulously. 'I thought I'd have to go to hospital—that's amazing! It doesn't hurt at all now!'

'I told you!' Rosie laughed. Her eye caught Andy's and he winked at her.

'When it comes to medical emergencies, we don't make a bad team, do we?' he murmured, holding her gaze.

There was something in his tone that seemed to be more than a professional comment. Rosie coloured slightly and quickly took a gauze pad from a cabinet and wound it gently round the nail.

'The pinprick in your nail will heal very quickly—I've just put this on to protect it for a few hours.'

'Thank you so much, both of you,' gabbled Veronica, her face a much healthier colour than when she'd come in. 'I'll collect Amy from Reception now.'

'You're sure you're OK?'

'Oh, yes, I'm fine. It's like a great big throbbing balloon's gone from my finger! It's really comfortable—I just can't believe it. We're going to the park now to feed the ducks and see the farm animals—Amy loves doing that!'

They all walked out to Reception and Maria brought a rather chocolate bedaubed little girl to the front.

'Amy definitely likes the chocolate biscuits best, don't you, love?'

Amy's little cheeks dimpled. 'More?' she said hopefully. 'Just one?' She looked longingly after Maria as she went back behind the glass in Reception.

'I don't think so, Amy.' Rosie chuckled. 'Why don't you go with Veronica—her finger's all better now—and tell the ducks in the park where you've been?'

Amy grabbed Veronica's hand and nodded eagerly. 'Come on, 'Ronica, see ducks!'

Andy bent down to the toddler's level. 'Would you like to take this little doll to see the ducks as well?' he asked, taking a small knitted woollen doll out of his pocket. 'She's never seen the ducks before!'

A chubby hand reached out to take the toy, and shining eyes looked up at him. 'Yes!' Amy shouted happily. Andy ruffled her hair affectionately and, watching him, Rosie had the sudden illogical feeling that he would make a wonderful father, the kind of father Tony might have been for Amy if he'd lived—kind, loving and gentle. She swallowed hard, suppressing an unwarranted feeling of tears prickling at the back of her eyes, and watched Amy toddling happily out with Veronica, cuddling the little doll to her body.

'That was kind,' she murmured. 'Do you keep a supply of those?'

Andy laughed. 'An elderly patient used to knit them for me—I have quite a stockpile!' He folded his arms and leant against the wall. 'Amy's a little sweetheart—you must be very proud of her.' He paused for a moment, his eyes narrowing slightly, then added softly, 'Any more little secrets you've kept from me?'

Rosie looked up at him sharply. 'What do you mean?' She frowned. 'Amy's not a secret—I didn't tell you about her because—'

'Because it might have frightened me off—or you didn't want to be reminded of your responsibilities?' A half-smile played around his lips.

'I don't know what you mean. It…it just never occurred to me, that's all.' Her voice sounded defensive, and embarrassed. She brushed a tendril of hair from her eyes. Wasn't it true that those thoughts *had* floated round her head that evening they'd met? She'd wanted to be fancy-free that night—a single unencumbered girl once more!

'I...I just didn't think it necessary to tell you every-thing about me,' she added carefully.

He nodded and said softly, 'I understand—really, I do.'

A flush of anger touched her cheeks. 'No, you don't,' she said heatedly. 'I adore Amy. She's the cen-tre of my life—not that it's any business of yours any-way. The day we met was the first time I'd been to a function by myself for a long time, and sometimes it's good to forget about one's home life for a while.' Then she added with more spirit, 'Anyway, why should you be interested in the trials and tribulations of bringing up a child alone? Occasionally it's refreshing to think of yourself for once, even though you love them so much. But you couldn't possibly appreciate that!'

'Why do you think that, Rosie?'

She frowned. There was something about his tone that caught her attention momentarily. She shrugged. 'I just mean that you can't have any idea of the joys, yes, and the heartbreak there are in being a parent.'

'Perhaps I do have an inkling, you know...'

Rosie looked at him sharply. 'Well, I just assumed that as you don't...'

'Have any children?' he finished off for her. He bunched his fists into his pockets and smiled faintly. 'Well, you're wrong in your assumption.' He paused for a second, then added slowly, 'It so happens I do have a son who means more than anything else in the world to me—so I think I know something of what you're talking about!' He added dryly, 'I used to have a wife as well, but she and I are no longer together.'

A blush of embarrassment rose up Rosie's face. How could she have been so arrogant as to suppose that she was the only one who had any knowledge of the trials of bringing up children and of being a lone parent?

'I…I'm so sorry… I hadn't realised…'

Andy laughed. 'Why should you? Obviously we both wanted to feel "free", as it were, the other night, and not admit to our other lives. And why shouldn't we forget our responsibilities for a short time, and keep our backgrounds to ourselves?'

The phone jangled loudly in Reception and at the same time a troop of people came through the surgery door for the baby clinic in the afternoon. Maria leaned over the counter and called, 'Dr Loveday—your first patient's arrived!'

Andy looked down at Rosie, a wry smile on his face. 'Maybe the reception area isn't quite the right place to have a heart-to-heart. We'll have to save that episode for another time—perhaps over a bottle of wine in more private surroundings!'

Rosie watched him as he walked out through the door. She wasn't sure that having a cosy tête-à-tête with Andy was wise, but she longed to find out more about his background, intrigued about his little boy and the child's mother. Her assumptions about him had been so naïve—she might have known that an attractive man like him would have someone in his background who would always come first.

She sighed. Although she'd made it clear to Andy that socialising was out of the question now that they worked together, suddenly she wanted to know very much indeed about everything in this man's life!

CHAPTER FOUR

LOOKING for a birthday present for Aunt Lily wasn't easy in a seething department store, where every counter seemed to have long queues—especially when one's mind was distracted! Pashminas and scarves danced before Rosie's eyes, mixed with thoughts of Andy and revelations about his son.

She picked up a beautiful scarlet pashmina which she was sure Lily would love, and sighed crossly. Why was the man crowding her thoughts so much? Since the first day he'd joined the surgery, it had been a shock to realise that, despite their unfortunate start, she could be attracted to a man so forcibly again, and to feel once more the erratic lurches of emotion she'd felt when she'd first met Tony.

'Do you want this gift-wrapped, madam?' The assistant's face swam into focus and for a second pushed out the image of a tousle-headed man with incredible sexy blue eyes.

Rosie shot a look at her watch—she had to cram as much as she could into her free afternoon before picking Amy up.

'No...no, I'll do it later myself, thanks.'

She paid for the pashmina hastily, and made her way through the crowds towards the lifts. If she was quick she'd have time to go to a little boutique round the corner and perhaps indulge herself in a new trouser suit for work. No point in getting anything for after-hours, she thought gloomily. The only person she truly wanted to ask her out was off-limits now they worked together, and she'd told him that in no uncertain terms!

The lift was rather full but Rosie found a small space at the side. Just as the doors were closing, a figure hurtled in, squashing close against her—a familiar tall figure, far too large for the amount of space left. She stared incredulously at Andy as he squeezed in beside her, and drew in a sharp breath as their bodies jammed together in the crowd, the roughness of his chin almost grazing her forehead. He seemed to have sprung from nowhere!

'Ah!' he murmured breathlessly. 'At last I've caught up with you. I've been trailing you for ages since I saw you across the store, but you were rather elusive!' He smiled at her, his blue eyes dancing a few inches away from hers. 'Wanted to organise that evening together I mentioned the other day. We have some talking to do. What do you think?'

Rosie looked dazedly up at him. It was as if by thinking about him, the man had actually materialised!

'What are you doing here?' she managed to gasp.

His eyes gleamed with amusement at her. 'Following you! Now, tell me what your thoughts are regarding a nice relaxing evening out!'

Any thoughts Rosie had at that particular moment were jumbled ones of Andy holding her very closely on a dark shore a few nights ago. She didn't want to be reminded of that...

She flicked a look round at the other people in the lift. Although Andy was keeping his voice fairly low, she could see interested faces towards her.

'That would be very nice some time,' she replied primly.

He grinned down at her. 'Come on, now,' he urged.

'What kind of relationship are we going to have if we don't get to know each other properly?'

'We…we haven't got a relationship,' she muttered. 'I told you—work before socialising!'

'Ah, yes—what was it you said? "You can't mix sex and business!" Was that it?'

Rosie was acutely aware of every eye in the lift swivelling their way.

'I meant it,' she snapped.

'Then what about a strictly platonic dinner tonight?' he pressed on, unabashed.

'I can't—no babysitter!' She wasn't going to use Lily as a convenient backstop whenever she needed to go out.

'Get one for tomorrow night, then!'

The lift jolted to a halt and people began to file out, flicking fascinated glances at the two of them as they left. Rosie gave a sigh of relief and made to step towards the doors. Andy's arm came in front of her and pressed the third-floor button. The doors closed and the lift started to move.

'Do you mind?' she protested. 'I've got to pick Amy up soon…'

'It's difficult to get you by yourself,' he explained gruffly as they sailed upwards, alone in the lift. 'Surgery meetings don't seem the right place to arrange dates, but I do feel that as we seemed to get off on rather a rocky footing the other day, we ought to put things right. I said some things I regretted very much, which I know hurt you—can't we make a fresh start by having dinner together?'

Rosie swallowed. Part of her longed to find out more about Andy in a quiet setting, but part of her was intensely apprehensive about starting anything again with this man!

'I really don't know,' she said stiffly. 'Now, would you mind taking this lift to the ground floor and letting me out? I'm wasting time.'

'Wait a minute, Rosie.' His finger pressed the 'stop' button and the lift halted suddenly between floors, making Rosie stumble against him. His hand went round her waist to steady her, and that familiar panicky feeling of desire and need flooded through her at his electric touch.

'Start this lift immediately. You're…you're harassing me!' she said bitingly, trying to ignore the delicious sense of danger that fluttered through her body.

'Calm down! I only want to extract a promise from you before you rush off.'

'Get this lift moving, or I'll press the alarm bell!'

His head bent towards hers, those magnetic blue eyes holding her gaze, his mobile lips just a breath away from hers, and her heart clattered against her ribs at his proximity. 'Then say you'll come to dinner with me on Friday—you'll be able to get a babysitter by then surely.'

He was frighteningly persuasive, his deep voice sounding ultra-reasonable. 'We have to build bridges, Rosie, if we're to work together. We can't be as close as we were the other night and forget all about it— even if you do want us just to ''be friends'', as you put it.'

Perhaps he was right. After all, having a meal didn't mean a repeat of the night of the conference and they *were* colleagues, all of them contributing to the running of the practice. It didn't make sense to be too distant.

She bit her lip, frightened yet excited by what Andy might do next if she refused to go out with him.

Reluctantly she nodded her head. 'You're nothing but a bully but, yes, all right, I will go out for a quick meal. And now take this darn thing down to the ground floor!'

As soon as the doors opened she marched out, feeling a mixture of annoyance and amusement. The cheek of it! Then she gave a gurgle of laughter. How could he choose a crowded lift to make a date with her? She took a deep breath of fresh air as she left the store and waited to cross the road. She wasn't being honest with herself, she thought wryly. Of course she wanted to go out with the man—every fibre of her longed to be close to him again, and to find out more about him.

'A friendly supper, nothing more,' she muttered to herself.

Friday was a mad day, starting with a hysterical mother convinced that her child had meningitis, interspersed with people asking for sick notes who weren't sick and genuinely ill people who needed specialist help. Rosie took a long sip of scalding coffee in the office and leant her head for a second against the glass partition. The day was going far too fast, roaring inexorably towards her date with Andy!

Why on earth had she agreed to this idiotic meal with him? It wasn't necessary—she didn't want or need to know anything more about the man, she said firmly to herself. She would make it a very short encounter and stick to very safe subjects—like the weather and work!

'Looking forward to tonight, Rosie. I've chosen quite a good place, I think!' Andy strode through

Reception with a sheaf of papers in his hand, a picture of vitality. 'I'll pick you up about seven-thirty—wrap up well in waterproof clothing!'

Rosie jumped slightly. 'Waterproof what?'

But Andy had swept out, tossing a bundle of papers in Maria's out-tray, leaving an impression of energy and...excitement? Rosie looked after him, anxiety and anticipation churning round in her stomach.

'I should never have agreed to it!' she repeated to herself.

Maria came into the office, looking apologetic. 'I know you've had a long list, but would you see Arabelle Carter? She's just come in and seems really agitated. Won't give me a clue as to what's wrong— just begs to be seen as soon as possible.'

Rosie sighed and looked pointedly at her watch. 'Oh, Lord—I'm brain-dead, Maria, but perhaps I've enough energy to see someone who's going to throw a wobbly!'

Maria went out of the room to tell the patient, and Rosie went into her room and brought up the woman's notes on the screen. Talk about excited and nervy— that was just how she felt! Perhaps, she thought wryly, she and Mrs Carter could exchange symptoms.

She peered forward and looked at Arabelle Carter's history. She was a woman of thirty-six who rarely used the practice—the last time had been about two years ago after some spotting between her periods caused by a small polyp which she'd had removed.

Rosie pressed the button on her desk that lit up the electronic sign in the surgery for the next patient, and in a few seconds the woman walked in.

Arabelle Carter was thin and tall, with mousy hair drawn back in a ponytail and large glasses—she had a rather studious, earnest look. She was elegantly and expensively dressed in a beautifully cut tan trouser suit, with gold chains round her neck and one wrist, but there was an air of vulnerability about her.

She sat bolt upright on the chair in front of Rosie's desk, clasping her hands tightly together. Her cheeks looked flushed and her eyes were wide and excited.

'Thank you so much for seeing me, Dr Loveday,' she started. 'I...I wouldn't have bothered you, but I'm so confused—I just don't know what to think! I should have made an appointment, but my husband's taking me away unexpectedly tomorrow, and I just couldn't wait until we got back—I'd go mad!'

'Well, perhaps you can tell me what's confusing you,' said Rosie.

'I think...I hope...I'm pregnant,' Arabelle began haltingly. 'You see, I've been married six years and I've wanted a baby for so long—but nothing happened. I was getting desperate.'

'But you never sought medical help?'

Arabelle looked down at her hands, twisting them nervously in her lap. 'Justin—that's my husband—he doesn't really want any more children. He has two teenagers by his first marriage and he says he's done his bit!' The girl gave a faint laugh. 'He's quite a lot older than me, and can't bear the thought of nappies and teenage years again, I suppose!'

'But now you think you're pregnant—have you done a test?'

Arabelle was silent for a second. 'I daren't,' she whispered. 'Justin thinks I'm on the Pill, but I came off it two years ago. If I am pregnant he'll know I've deceived him, and if I'm not I'll be devastated!' There

was a pause and then she added rather fiercely, 'But I
know I am!'

'Have your periods stopped?'

'Since I stopped taking the Pill they've always been
very scanty. It's just that I'm absolutely huge! I can
feel the baby there—really big and round. Nothing fits
and I have to keep dashing to the loo!'

'I'd like to do a pregnancy test, Mrs Carter, and then
give you a quick examination. I shall do a test on your
urine and we should have the result pretty soon after
I've felt your tummy. I don't tend to do internal pelvic
examinations at an early stage of pregnancy.'

Rosie palpated the woman's stomach. The bump in
Arabelle Carter's uterus was easy to feel, but it didn't
feel quite like a growing foetus—it was a hard, un-
malleable mass. When she'd finished she was almost
sure that the reason for her patient's enlarged uterus
wasn't pregnancy.

'Have you felt sick at all?' she asked Arabelle. The
woman shook her head.

'No—nothing like that. I've always had a good appetite. Perhaps I'm a bit tired.'

'While you get dressed again, I'll just see what result
the pregnancy test kit gives.'

Rosie dipped the indicator stick in the test tube con-
taining the urine and test solution, then held the stick
up. As she'd suspected, there was no change in colour
on the indicator strips. She turned to the young woman
now sitting in the chair by her desk.

'Mrs Carter...' she said gently.

'Oh, please, call me Arabelle,' said the woman eagerly. 'It seems less formal somehow.'

'Arabelle, then.' Rosie sighed inwardly. It was hard
giving bad news to patients but there was no getting

away from it. 'From my examination of you and the results of the test kit, it doesn't look as if you are pregnant.'

Arabelle stared at her in shocked astonishment. 'But…but, Dr Loveday, I must be! Even I can feel the bump! Sometimes those kits aren't accurate—you can't rely on them!'

Rosie looked at her sympathetically. 'That's true— they say a negative result is about eighty per cent accurate—but I'm going on more physical evidence than that, and from feeling your tummy and the unyielding feel of the mass there I'd say that you're probably suffering from fibroids.'

'What do you mean? What are they?'

'Well, they consist of bundles of muscles which form a benign tumour—that is, not cancerous. But they can get pretty big and distort the uterus. Sometimes they cause heavy periods—unusually not in your case evidently—but they may press on your bladder and they can cause back pain. They can also prevent pregnancy or cause miscarriages.'

'So what can be done?' Arabelle looked scared, her eyes large and frightened behind her studious-looking glasses.

'To confirm my diagnosis I'll send you for an ultrasound scan—and if I'm correct a gynaecologist will assess whether you should have an operation to remove them.'

There was a short silence, then Arabelle gave a choking cry and looked at Rosie with tear-filled eyes. 'I…I won't have to have to have a hysterectomy, will I? I couldn't bear that! There'd be no hope then!' She bit her lip and passed a hand over her forehead. 'I'm sorry,' she whispered. 'It's hard to come to terms with this.'

Rosie got up and patted her comfortingly on the shoulder. 'I know it's a shock to come in thinking you might be pregnant and then be told it's something completely different, but if you do have to have an operation, it's usually very successful—and it's a last resort to have a hysterectomy. There are other techniques nowadays. Sometimes the fibroid can be shelled out from its capsule without damage to the uterus.'

'Would it mean I could get pregnant then?'

'You might have a better chance,' said Rosie cautiously.

Arabelle shook her head. 'I can't believe it,' she whispered. 'I was so sure... All the women my age seem to have children and I was beginning to feel left out.' She smiled palely. 'I feel as if I'm running out of time, and the longer I leave it, the less Justin will be able to accept it when I do get pregnant!'

Rosie leant back against the desk and looked thoughtfully at Arabelle. 'Don't you think it would be wise to talk to your husband?' she suggested. 'Does he know how you feel—how much you'd like a child?'

Arabelle shrugged rather hopelessly. 'I have tried, but he's very evasive on the subject. He's quite a powerful character and very volatile—and he did tell me before we got married that he didn't want to be a father again. I didn't realise I'd start getting so broody, and I suppose I'm frightened of causing a row.' She gave a shaky little laugh. 'I'm afraid I do anything for a peaceful life! Not that it is all that peaceful,' she sighed, and dabbed at her eyes with a handkerchief.

'Is there anything else you want to tell me?' probed Rosie delicately, looking sharply at the bleak-looking girl before her. 'Are things, er…all right between you and your husband otherwise?'

Arabelle sniffed. 'Oh, yes—I adore him. It's his teenage children that can be a little difficult.'

For 'little difficult' read 'bloody impossible', thought Rosie astutely. 'They live with you, then?'

The girl nodded and said sadly, 'Most of the time they're with us. I have tried hard to understand them, but they resent me very much. Justin doesn't realise how difficult they can be with me—in front of him they're fine!'

Rosie looked at her sympathetically. 'Looks like you'll have to have a real heart-to-heart with your husband. You'll tell him if you have to have an operation, I take it?'

'Yes…yes, I'd have to do that, I suppose.'

Arabelle got up from the chair, smoothing her jacket down and looking distracted. 'Justin's awfully busy—his work demands all his time so I try not to worry him with details.'

'This is hardly a detail,' commented Rosie gently. 'I'm sure he'd want to know. I'll write a letter to the consultant and you'll get details of an appointment sent to you. I'd like to see you again when he gives his verdict. And, Arabelle, try not to worry. It may all turn out for the best—and perhaps on your holiday you can talk to your husband about your worries.'

Rosie frowned to herself as she input Arabelle Carter's notes into the computer. The Carters' marriage seemed an odd relationship—it was almost as if Arabelle was frightened of her powerful husband, and that he was less than sensitive. Reading between the lines, it seemed that Arabelle Carter was being domi-nated on all sides—not least by two teenage stepchildren! She hoped the woman would get the support from her husband she needed over the next few weeks.

She flicked a look at her watch and groaned. Nearly six o'clock! The hour and a half before Andy picked her up would have to go like oiled clockwork! Feed Amy, put her to bed, then a bath for herself and a search for something reasonable to wear. Rosie's stomach did a somersault. She couldn't deny she was excited—and apprehensive. 'Just like a teenager on her first date,' she muttered scornfully to herself as she drove away from the surgery.

Amy was playing on the sitting-room floor surrounded by her noisiest toys—little trains that whistled and rang bells, boxes that made the sounds of animals when you pressed the right picture and a plastic telephone that emitted a shrill ringing tone. Lily was in the garden, watching her small charge through the open window and drawing heavily on a cigarette.

'Hello, darling!' she called. 'Sorry, I just had to have a smoke after the day I've had. That's why I'm out here—so Amy won't notice!' She stubbed her cigarette out and flicked it into the flower-bed. Rosie smiled. It was difficult for Lily to change the habit of a lifetime, but at least she didn't do it near Amy.

'Why—has your day been so awful?' she asked, gathering Amy up in her arms and kissing her soft cheek.

Lily came in through the French windows and sighed. 'The autumn collection has come in, but naturally with this boiling weather people are still looking for lightweight stuff. I've got a sale going on at one end of the shop and new things fighting for space at the other end. And, of course, I'm trying to get the fashion show under way. And wouldn't you know it—

two of the models I use are heavily pregnant, and the pianist I use for elegant background music is going on some tour!'

'Very inconsiderate of them!' Rosie laughed, taking Amy into the kitchen and putting her in her high chair. Lily's fashion show was a major event every year, raising a huge amount for charity and demanding an immense amount of preparation. 'You look tired, Lily. You have got something in for supper this evening—something nutritious?'

Lily probably owed her reed-slim frame to a complete disinterest in food. 'Yes, yes, darling,' she said impatiently. 'Don't fuss! I think a quick gin and tonic might help at the moment!'

She poured herself a generous glass and watched Rosie butter thin soldiers of bread for Amy and mash the contents of a boiled egg into a little dish. 'What time are you off gallivanting with this young man?' she enquired.

'About seven-thirty—hardly gallivanting! It's only a quick meal. He's a locum and I'm going to answer any questions he might have about the practice. We've all been so busy that the evening seemed a good time to do it.'

Rosie did her best to sound casual, as if the whole thing was rather a bore and not of much consequence, but she couldn't help a self-conscious blush colour her cheeks.

'And what are you going to wear?' asked Lily with interest.

'Oh—he said I had to wear waterproofs!'

'Waterproofs?' Lily looked scandalised. 'Where on earth are you eating—on a lifeboat? Oh, I do like you to look nice when you go out—you've such a lovely figure and, heaven knows, you don't get taken out to dinner much.'

'I've told you, Lily, it's just a working supper. It doesn't matter what I look like!'

Lily sniffed. 'It certainly does. I shall want to see that you look really smart under those waterproofs!'

After the usual 'three bears' story, Amy was snuggled down into bed. 'Mummy out?' she said sleepily.

'Just for a little while, darling—Auntie Lily will be here. I'll come in and see you when I get back.'

Rosie looked down at the wild curls spread over the pillow and the long lashes fanned out on the chubby cheek—whatever would she do without her little girl? If only Tony could see how beautiful and sweet she was. But, of course, the one thing she couldn't do for her was to bring back her father...

Her wardrobe revealed nothing much that Lily would regard as 'very smart', Rosie thought gloomily. It was a very warm evening, so in the end she put on a light ice-blue silk shirt with a pair of cream linen trousers. It looked and felt cool, the colour of the shirt flattering to her warm skin tones. She would take a mac with her, but she was darned if she was going to put it on at the start of the evening!

The front doorbell rang just as she finished sweeping her hair up in a knot at the back of her head and putting on a touch of lipstick and a light eye-shadow—enough to hide the end-of-day weariness that looked back at her from the mirror. She heard Lily's practised social tones greeting Andy, and quickly ran downstairs before her aunt had given him the third degree—she loved to know everything about everyone!

Andy was talking to Lily as Rosie peeped round the

door of the little living room. A feeling of a hundred butterflies fluttering in her stomach made her stop for a moment. Heavens, but the man was gorgeous! Perhaps it was his unusual colouring of thick tawny hair and his broad frame exuding confidence and energy that made the room look small and crowded. Whatever, his presence in her own home sent shock waves through her. She swallowed. Remember, Rosie, she said sternly to herself, this is purely a polite social evening to put things on a friendly basis between us so that we can work well together…

He turned as she came in, his eyes sweeping over her tall slender figure then holding her eyes for a microsecond. 'I was just telling your aunt that you and I actually met last weekend at the conference, and how extraordinary it was that I should then turn up as a locum at the practice!'

Lily looked reproachfully at her. 'You never told me that you'd met anyone as handsome as Andy at the weekend—just that you'd been abseiling!'

'Ah,' remarked Andy, his eyes twinkling wickedly at Rosie, 'I obviously didn't register much with your niece, then!'

Rosie shot him a baleful look—how dared he tease her? She knew Lily was far too perceptive to miss any frisson between the two of them. 'I think we should go now,' she said quickly. 'I can't stay too long—I've promised Amy I'll look in on her when we get back.'

'You stay out as long as you like!' declared Lily. 'I shall have a lovely evening watching all the soaps that are on tonight!'

Andy smiled at Lily. 'I'll take care of her,' he said pleasantly and, putting a proprietorial arm round Rosie, shepherded her out to his car.

'Where are we going that I should need a mac?' she asked as she clipped on her seat belt. Her hands fumbled slightly as she did it up. Why couldn't she treat this evening as she'd told Lily it would be—a casual evening out with a colleague? She felt as tense as a violin string, the events of the conference weekend still running vividly in her mind like the rewind of a video, and she couldn't believe that Andy wasn't thinking of that, too!

'You'll find out where we're going in a few minutes,' Andy said mysteriously, swinging the car onto the road and taking the route that led inland along the river. He flicked a glance across at her. 'Busy day?' he asked.

Rosie snatched gratefully at the mundane remark—it was safe to talk about work, thank goodness!

'Fairly. Just as I was finishing, a patient came in, hoping she was pregnant—I had to tell her I thought she had fibroids. She was pretty upset—feels her biological time clock's ticking away, and doesn't think her husband would be keen on a new baby anyway as he's got teenagers from a previous marriage.'

'Sounds pretty complicated,' commented Andy.

'She's got a lot to deal with. It can't be easy for her, looking after children who resent her.'

Andy nodded grimly. 'Perhaps it's not easy for the children either,' he said tersely. 'It works both ways, you know.'

Rosie flicked a quick look of surprise at him—there was something in his voice that indicated Andy felt rather deeply about this particular subject. Before she had time to question him, he drew the car into the side of the road by the river.

'Here we are,' he announced. 'Time to put on your raincoat now!'

Rosie peered out of the car window. She hadn't been in the area all that long, so didn't know too much of the surrounding countryside. She drew in a gasp of surprised delight. A waterfall tumbled down the cliff into the river, and high on the hill to the side of it perched a restaurant with a balcony overlooking the sparkling cascade of water.

'Wow!' she murmured in awe. 'That is spectacular!'

Andy took her arm as they climbed the steps. 'Now you know why we need waterproofs when we have a drink. If the wind blows, you can get drenched from the spray!'

On the balcony of the restaurant, Rosie looked across at the waterfall in delight. Although the sun was fairly low in the sky, its rays touched the spray and a faint rainbow arced across to the steps below her. In the distance, the sea was a blue wash, and the sky above it tinged with the faintest of rose pinks. She gazed at it, entranced, drinking in the balmy air and the faint smell of woodsmoke that drifted up the cliffside.

'It'll be a nice day tomorrow, I guess,' said Andy, coming up behind her and handing her an exotic-looking drink with fruit floating on the top. 'I think you'll find this refreshing after a hard day's work,' he commented. 'It's got all kinds of relaxing things in it—guaranteed to make you forget all things medical!'

They didn't talk for a while—the noise of the cascading water made it impossible. Rosie sipped her drink and felt whatever was in it making its way speedily to her empty stomach. The tensions of the day began to ease, and the nervousness she'd had about the

evening started to float away. Andy glanced at her
flushed cheeks and sparkling eyes and laughed.

'Feeling better? Perhaps it's time for a little food.'

Rosie nodded rather dizzily, a light-headed sensation
beginning to hit her rather pleasantly. Somehow the
evening was turning out to be less daunting than she'd
imagined. Perhaps she and Andy could be friends
after all!

CHAPTER FIVE

THEY sat next to a huge picture window which looked out on the spectacular view. Rosie looked round the room with delight—the discreet golden lighting and arched ceiling with stars pinpricked in tiny lights all over it made her feel she was floating in the sky. She settled back in her chair and felt the convivial atmosphere, with the low murmuring voices and soft music in the background, wash over her. It was a long time since she'd felt so relaxed.

'This is wonderful. I never even knew The Cascades existed. I haven't had the opportunity to get to know the area very well yet.' She smiled across at Andy. 'I have to admit I feel very hungry!'

'That's good.' His blue eyes were navy in the darker light of the restaurant, but she could see the humorous gleam in their depths. 'I like to see a girl enjoy her food!'

Rosie bit into a succulent piece of subtly spiced salmon *en croute*, and reflected that maybe it *was* possible to enjoy herself on an occasional evening out—life didn't have to be all responsibility and worry—just as long as she kept things inconsequential!

Andy leant back and looked at her appraisingly. 'I like your hair up like that,' he murmured softly, 'There's something rather...Edwardian about it!'

'It's cool on a warm evening like this,' she replied lightly. 'I hope it doesn't make me look too forbidding!'

'No, although there's something rather attractive about an ice-maiden!' He grinned, and refilled her glass. 'Now, tell me—how did you come to be in this part of the world?'

In the intimate atmosphere of the restaurant, and relaxed with the unaccustomed wine, Rosie found it easy to talk to Andy. She told him about her uncle and how he'd left his cottage to her, so that his sister Lily could live with them.

'Lily's always been on her own, never married. She runs this brilliant dress shop, but now she's older Uncle Bart was worried about the future for her. She's a wonderful woman and marvellous with Amy.'

Andy listened closely, watching her face intently, noting the flush on her cheeks and her sparkling eyes when she spoke of her little daughter.

'What about the rest of your family—parents, brothers or sisters?' he asked.

She sighed. 'I'm an only child and my parents sadly died some years ago—that's why it was so great that Uncle Bart left me this lovely place to live. I felt I could make a new start here after Tony died. After all, I had no family to keep me in the North of England.'

'You've certainly picked a lovely part of the world. I'd love to show you some of the little coves and bays I used to explore when I was a boy.'

Rosie took a sip of wine. She wasn't sure about the long-term implication of that. Then she shrugged inwardly. Wasn't she being a little bit paranoid, frightened of being hurt and abandoned if they established a relationship?

She put down her knife and fork and smiled across at him. 'I've told you all about myself,' she said. 'You must be bored stiff with me doing my boastful mum act about Amy—not really your scene, I'm sure! Let's change the subject—tell me about your little boy.'

He gave a faint smile and picked up his wineglass, twirling it absently and watching the dark red liquid swirl around, catching the light. 'It's hard to know where to begin,' he said slowly. 'I'll give you the edited version, I think!'

Rosie looked at him curiously. 'It sounds as if you have quite a story to tell!'

'I don't normally bore people about my private life, but when I learned about Amy I realised that perhaps you and I might have a very special understanding of each other's problems.' He paused for a second, then remarked wryly. 'You said the other day that I couldn't possibly identify with the worries of being a parent.'

Rosie blushed slightly—she didn't want to be reminded of making such a crass and arrogant remark. Andy reached into his breast pocket and brought out a photograph which he passed over the table to her. She found herself looking at a picture of a solemn-faced little boy of about seven—a beautiful child with dark russet hair and large blue eyes.

'This is Keiron,' Andy said quietly and with evident pride. 'He's my son. He's my priority and I love him very much. I try to see him as often as I can, although sometimes it's not easy. A child should have two loving parents who look after him together, if that's at all possible.'

There was a sad timbre to Andy's voice, and a lot of heartbreak behind his remarks.

Rosie said quietly, 'He's a lovely-looking boy. Does he live near you, then?'

He shook his head. 'Keiron lives with his mother in

the States. At least,' he murmured, 'you see your little girl every day and can watch her growing up.'

He stared out at the gathering dusk. 'I wanted his happiness and stability to come before everything else,' he said slowly. 'I'd sacrifice anything for that—and for various reasons I think it better that he stays with his mother.'

There was a hush between them. The low murmur of voices intermingled with soft music in the background, but Andy's words seemed to echo round the room.

Rosie studied the tense lines of Andy's good-looking face in the muted light of the restaurant. He had just as many worries as she had—probably more, with his child so far away. A well of sympathy rose inside her— at least she had Amy living with her and Lily to confide in. Why had she imagined that she had been the only one with a troubled life? There were so many things about Andy Templeton that she didn't know.

'I'm so sorry,' she said at last, then added gently, 'Did you meet his mother in the States?'

Andy shook his head. 'Sonia was a nurse in the hospital I trained at in London, but she came from Chicago. We got married over here but when we broke up she wanted to go back to her family in the States... She had been very homesick and there was no way she'd stay here.'

'And Keiron went with her? That must have been very hard for you—and Keiron, too, I guess.'

He gave a faint sardonic smile. 'You've no idea how heartbreaking it was—but there was no way my son was going to be a tug-of-love child, each parent going to court for custody. I was determined that Keiron wouldn't be like a little football, kicked back and forth between his mother and father.'

There was a fiercely harsh tone to his voice—as if there were more reasons than most for him to protect his son.

'That was quite a sacrifice,' said Rosie compassionately.

His eyes met hers over the table. 'Having a child yourself, you'll understand that I couldn't bear to see Keiron unhappy. I try and remain on good terms with Sonia, and I go and see him as often as I can—of course, that takes a lot of time. It's a good job we didn't have more children—one is more than enough to cope with!'

Of course she could understand that all Andy's energies would be taken up with his son. She herself had always hoped for more children some day—companions for Amy. As an only child herself, she'd always longed for brothers or sisters. Although she could understand Andy's point of view, she was vaguely surprised. He seemed to have a wonderful rapport with children, and she guessed he made a wonderful father.

'You decided not to follow them to the States and work there?'

'On the face of it, that might have been a good idea—but there were a number of difficulties. I still had exams to take and I didn't want to compromise my future or Keiron's by missing out on those.'

'And that's why you don't want to tie yourself down to a permanent job?'

'At the moment, yes.'

And that, thought Rosie, smiling wryly to herself, is why you will always remain fancy-free. No room for permanent relationships when you have such heavy commitments far away. She stared out of the window at the gathering twilight, the waterfall now looking like a silver ribbon shimmering against the dark cliff. Even more reason not to get entangled with him, she reflected sternly. She would be the one that would get hurt when his son needed him.

His eyes looked across at her with something of their old humour. 'What are you thinking of?' he prompted her.

The words seemed to hang in the air before Rosie. He was free to have a fling when he wanted, but his son would always claim first allegiance.

She took a gulp of wine. 'It's very hard for you,' she said at last.

He smiled, as if in reassurance. 'I don't want you to think it's all doom and gloom. Keiron lives in a lovely part of the States and we have a wonderful time when I go over—although it would be nice to have someone else to share him with when we go on our outings. Sonia goes off on holiday when I arrive. Perhaps it's for the best.'

'So do you manage to remain friendly when you see her?'

He was silent, then he shrugged his shoulders. 'Sonia's a good mother or I couldn't have let Keiron go. Things between us were OK, reasonably amicable, but I heard some news from her the other day. It gave me a jolt, I have to admit.'

'It wasn't good news, then?'

'I had a phone call from her the morning I was due to meet you at the conference. She informed me she was getting married again, to a man I suspected she was having an affair with when we were married.'

'That must have been terrible for you...'

Andy shrugged. 'I'm afraid he was one of many diversions she had. He's very much older than her—old enough to be her father, in fact.'

'So what was the attraction?'

Andy grinned ruefully. 'I imagine a great deal of wealth, and the fact that he's a peer of the realm! Sonia would find being called "Lady Forester" irresistible!'

Rosie looked at him perceptively. 'And the fact she's marrying this man worries you?'

He frowned. 'Of course. He could never feel for Keiron as I do.' He looked at the photo of his son. 'As I said before, a child should have two loving parents if possible—parents committed to that child's welfare.' Then he added with a wry smile, 'And preferably not living four thousand miles apart. This man may be OK, but how do I know how he'll be with my son—or how Keiron will take to him? I don't know if he needs someone new in his life right now.'

Yet another reason for Andy to steer clear of a permanent relationship, reflected Rosie. How would his son take to his father having a girlfriend? There was a short silence between them. It wasn't hard to imagine how heart-breaking the whole situation was, and Rosie's expression said as much. As if he knew what she was thinking, his hand came across the table and placed it over hers, warm and strong—a comforting feeling really.

'Thank you for listening to my tale of woe.' He smiled. 'It's good to talk to someone who knows what it's like to be a single parent. Strictly speaking, I don't fall into that category—but it feels as if I'm alone a lot of the time.'

Certain scenes rushed vividly back to Rosie—the night they'd met and she'd confided to Andy how

lonely she'd felt since Tony's death. Now the roles
were reversed... She trembled slightly. She only had
to think of that time and darts of desire flicked through
her as though her body remembered its close encounter
with his and how wonderfully they had melded together.

She tried to pull her hand back. It would be too easy
to fall back into that trap again and now, feeling sorry
for Andy, her defences would be lower than ever. She
longed to ask him more questions about himself and
his son, but his mood had changed. She sensed that he
had told her as much as he wanted for the time being,
and now it was time to move on to other subjects.

Rosie smiled at him. 'Tell me about your life here.
Have you always lived in this area?'

'Cornish—born and bred!' he said. 'At the moment
I live with my father and aunt—perhaps another thing
we have in common! My stepmother died some years
ago and my father is disabled, so my aunt looks after
him. I'd like to take you back to the house some day.
I think you'd be interested to see it—it's an old con-
verted coaching house with a few secret passages that
hid some smugglers in days gone past.'

'It sounds fantastic. Did you live there as a child?'

'Oh, yes—and Keiron loves it just as much as I do.
When we lived as a family here, he was always wanting to visit his grandfather and hear the tales he'd make
up about the rogues who used to roam these parts. I'm
hoping... There's just a chance that I can bring Keiron
back here for a few weeks in the summer holidays and
let him explore the house again.'

In the muted light of the restaurant his face seemed
softer, less angular, and there was a boyish, more care-

free look about him when he spoke of the house he lived in and Keiron's delight in it.

'It sounds very intriguing, Andy—like something out of a Daphne du Maurier novel.'

His eyes sparkled at her. 'Exactly! We've even got a little cove on the beach at the end of the garden—it's wonderful!' He poured some more wine into her glass and looked at her with an impish gaze. 'Now, let's get onto more important things—what about some treacle tart with whipped cream?'

The adroit change of subject made Rosie laugh. 'I couldn't eat anything else. Just some coffee, I think, and then perhaps we'd better go. As I said, I promised Amy I'd look in on her when I got back.'

'Then why don't we skip coffee and you can make me some at the cottage?'

Her heart gave a warning thump against her ribs. Did she want to ask him back to the intimacy of the little sitting room—the two of them alone together? She knew Lily would have gone to bed—of course Amy would be asleep—and yet it would seem churlish to say no after they'd had such a lovely evening.

'Of course,' she said weakly. 'If you don't mind instant!'

Crossing the restaurant to leave, Rosie noticed a familiar face watching them. Arabelle Carter was sitting in a corner of the room with a distinguished-looking white-haired older man. She caught Rosie's eye and gave a rather embarrassed wave. Rosie smiled back at her.

'You know those people?' enquired Andy, steering her down the stairs to the car park.

'She was the patient I saw this evening—the one I

told you about who mistakenly thought she was pregnant, but I'm sure she's got fibroids.'

'They live fairly near me,' remarked Andy, opening the car door for her. 'I see him quite often in the post office. Rather a dominating sort of chap—big booming voice, likes to make his opinion known.'

'Poor Arabelle,' sighed Rosie. 'I don't know if he'll listen sympathetically to her longing to have a baby. I only hope she won't have to have a hysterectomy.'

The golden glow of a lamp in the little sitting room was all that lit the cottage when they returned, otherwise it was in darkness. Lily had almost certainly gone to bed, thought Rosie apprehensively, leaving her alone with Andy. She flicked on the switch in the hallway and he closed the front door gently behind him. The hall looked tiny and cramped with his tall broad frame taking up most of the room.

'I'll go and put the kettle on.' Rosie moved swiftly to the kitchen. There was a definite 'danger zone' near Andy as far as she was concerned—anything nearer than three feet from him and that incredible physical attraction she'd felt for him when they'd first met seemed to come into play. Now, however, she knew something about his background and it was as if things had shifted to a more intimate footing—she felt the nervousness of someone on emotional quicksands.

When she came back to the sitting room with mugs of coffee, he was sitting on the settee, his long legs sprawled in front of him, a double photograph in his hand—Tony in one frame and Amy in the other.

'I do see a likeness between your husband and your daughter, although she's remarkably like you,' he said.

He looked up at Rosie sympathetically. 'He looks a good man. It's tragic he never saw his little girl.'

Rosie nodded, setting down the coffee on a little table. 'He would have been a great father, but Amy's never known what it's like to have a dad. She's going to grow up with a lot of female influence in her life, just Lily and me!'

'I don't think she'll come to any harm.' Andy stood up and put the photograph down, then looked quizzically at Rosie. 'Perhaps I could help add a masculine slant. How about me taking you all for a picnic in one of the little coves I knew when I was a boy? I'm a great sandcastle-builder, and Amy could bring a little friend. You see, Rosie—' He held her glance with those amazing clear blue eyes. 'I really do want to get to know you better—as a friend. And that includes your family. I may not have my son near me, but I can enjoy my friends' children.'

Rosie bit her lip and picked up her coffee. She put her hands round the mug as if to warm herself as a warning chill swept through her. Of course she couldn't object to having him as a friend. Heavens, she needed all the friends she could have in her position. But she was beginning to realise that on her side it could become much more than being good friends. Playing happy families on a beach could very soon turn to dependence and love on her part for a man she wasn't sure wanted a permanent relationship. It would be too easy to fall for someone like Andy Templeton. She moved to the window and looked out into the inky darkness.

'Perhaps,' she said, forcing her voice to sound light, 'when…when the sea warms up a little. I'm sure Amy would love that.'

'I hope you would love it, too, Rosie.' He had moved just behind her. She felt his hand on her shoulder and he turned her gently round, putting his hand under her chin and tilting her face towards his. 'What's the matter?' he said softly. 'I get the feeling you're keeping me at a distance.'

Rosie swallowed nervously. This was a delicate situation—she had to work with this man professionally, and yet all her senses were screaming at her to fling her arms round him and press her lips to his in a most unprofessional way! He was so close. It was hard to ignore the way her senses reacted to the clean, soapy, male smell of him, his powerful physical aura. She turned abruptly away and sat tensely on the edge of the little sofa.

'Don't be silly.' Her voice was rather breathless. 'As I said, it's a lovely idea of yours and of course we'll do it some time—look forward to it.'

He nodded slowly, his eyes sweeping slowly over her face, then he sat down on the chair near her and leant forward, a serious look in his eyes.

'You're frightened of something, Rosie,' he said gently. 'It's simple. We met, we liked each other, we had fun and then…then we had something more. We can't let that disappear…'

Rosie sprang up from her seat and moved to the fireplace. Too darn right she was afraid—afraid of her own passions. Why in heaven's name had she been such a fool as to allow this man to make love to her the first night they'd met? They were two lonely people, but it was obvious that he only needed short-term comfort until he went to see his son again. She would never come first with Andy.

'I don't want to talk about it now,' she said with a

catch in her voice. 'That was then, before I knew we were going to work together.' She added rather defiantly, 'You'll think I'm a bundle of complexes, but it just happens to be the way I think...'

Andy stood up and looked down at her, his eyes twinkling. 'That's all right—I like complicated women! But if you don't want to, we won't talk about it now.' He paused for a second then he gave a crooked little smile. 'But I can't believe, Rosie, that you don't feel something of what I feel.'

Rosie's heartbeat accelerated uncomfortably. 'I think we're on dangerous ground here, Andy,' she whispered. 'Remember what I said...'

His hand crept round her back and he pulled her towards him. 'It's your fault,' he murmured. 'You shouldn't look so darned beautiful.' His hands went behind her head and pulled out the combs holding her chignon, so that her thick hair sprang halo-like round her head. His fingers entwined themselves in the tendrils round her face and his face hovered above hers. 'I don't care if we do work together...' he whispered. 'Surely this can't be wrong.'

His lips descended on hers with soft butterfly kisses fluttering down her jawline to the hollow in her neck. Any second, thought Rosie hazily, he'll reach the point of no return and then I'll be lost! Her breasts felt heavy and full as a flash of unbelievable sexual response went through her, making her limbs lose their strength and her body melt against him.

She thought dizzily through a cloud of desire that she couldn't allow what had happened on their first meeting to happen again. How easy it would be to capitulate, to do what she really longed to do and blend her body with his, feel his hard, comforting warmth around her. She tried to concentrate on the little voice inside her head that insisted she was just a pleasant distraction from his troubles, and in the end she'd be the loser.

For a second she allowed his lips to tease hers apart, to feel the luxury of his arms pressing her against his hard muscular body, then with a tremendous effort of will she turned her head and twisted firmly away from him.

'Do you mind?' She tried to keep her voice lightly chiding—she didn't want to part on unfriendly terms with him. 'I think I've made myself reasonably clear about this!'

He stood back and laughed, his eyebrow raised in amusement. Rosie knew with a flash of embarrassment that he was just as aware of her eager response to his kisses as she had been. Then he pulled her gently but firmly to him again and tilted her head with his finger under her chin so that she was forced to look at him.

'What's the matter, Rosie? What's so different now to that magical time we had together last week? Why is it wrong now if it wasn't wrong then?'

He seemed to treat it as a bit of a joke, she thought dryly. She tried to keep her voice even. 'It wouldn't work, Andy. I told you before, we're colleagues now. Let's leave it at that, shall we?'

'Come on, now. Everyone needs to be desired, loved…' He paused, then said softly, a coaxing note in his voice, 'Perhaps we could be just…very good friends?'

What did he mean by that? Was it possible to be 'very good friends' and stop oneself falling in love? Having a platonic friendship with someone like

Andrew Templeton, who made her heart lurch every time she saw him, didn't seem possible to Rosie.

'I hope,' she replied primly, but with an edge of sharpness in her voice, 'that we can always be friendly colleagues…'

She stepped away from him, but he caught her hands in his and held her eyes for a moment. 'Then if that's what you want, let's try and start at that,' he said gently. 'I wouldn't want to do anything you wouldn't want me to… I'm sorry if I came on too strong.'

Rosie bit her lip. That was just the trouble. She *did* want him—oh, so much!

A sudden bumping sound against the door made them both jump apart. A little voice outside the room said plaintively, 'Mummy! Drink—please, drink!'

Rosie whipped round guiltily, then opened the door. Amy stood there, a plump little figure in pink pajamas with a large teddy bear in her arms. She smiled cheerfully at Rosie and Andy, her big brown eyes looking from one to the other.

'Biscuits, too?' she enquired hopefully.

Rosie rushed over to her and enveloped her in a hug, sweeping her up in her arms. 'Hello, darling,' she whispered into the child's neck, smelling the sweet baby smell of her. 'You've come in the nick of time—am I glad to see you!'

Andy watched mother and daughter cuddling each other with a rather wistful look on his face. It reminded him of when Keiron had been a baby, doing just the same thing and running to him for comfort in the night. What a wonderful feeling it had been to be needed and trusted. Seeing Amy with Rosie reinforced that feeling of isolation he had from his beloved little boy.

His throat constricted and he turned away from the

tender scene for a second. Perhaps, he thought gloomily, he had too much baggage from his past to make a long-term relationship with Rosie possible. Just because there was an incredible spark between them, it didn't mean she wanted him in her life permanently. She'd probably be rightly wary of a man with one failed marriage behind him...

The words an old nanny had used, when his natural impatience had overcome him as a boy, floated into his head: 'Make haste slowly, young man!'

Perhaps she was right, he reflected as his eyes followed Rosie carrying Amy out to the kitchen. She looked back at him as she went through the door.

'Could you let yourself out? It's getting late and it may take some time to get Amy back to sleep.'

'Sure,' he murmured. 'Don't worry, I'll go now.'

Amy gave him a little wave and a little cheeky grin over her mother's shoulder and Andy laughed, feeling himself relax—he couldn't give up on Rosie so easily. He'd take things more cautiously in future, learn to hold back—there was all the time in the world to build bridges.

'Time for me to go,' he murmured. He slipped out of the room and let himself quietly out.

CHAPTER SIX

TALK about a bad hair day! Everything that could go wrong seemed to have happened in the hour between getting up and having breakfast. Rosie looked ruefully at the washing machine and the large puddle of water that was spilling out of it onto the floor, getting larger every second. Why had it had to happen today when Lily had disappeared off to work early to try and organise some more models for her impending fashion show, and Amy was obviously sickening for a bad cold?

'And as for you,' she said crossly to Boggle, who was lying in his basket looking reflective, 'I don't know what Lily will say to you when she discovers you've chewed that lovely leather handbag of hers.'

Rosie sighed and flicked the 'off' switch of the washing machine. It made a hideous moaning noise and shuddered to a halt in mid-spin. Trust it to pack up at the weekend, when it would be difficult to get a plumber. She put a hand to her forehead. With everything happening all at once, and the tension of organising a washing machine, a child and a dog before work, she felt exhausted, and the slightly nauseous feeling she'd had all week seemed worse.

'I'm like a juggler,' she informed Boggle mournfully, 'trying to deal with hundreds of problems all by myself.'

Boggle slapped his tail politely against his basket, and Rosie felt a wave of self-pity wash over her. It helped to have the dear old dog to tell her troubles to, but he couldn't really offer any practical solutions! She and Amy had probably both got a virus—but she had to get into work somehow, whatever she felt like.

It was the Saturday morning emergency surgery: Ben was away for the weekend and there was no way she would ask Andy to fill in for her. It had been two weeks since their dinner date and Rosie had kept out of his way as much as she could. At the weekly practice meetings she'd sat at the end of the table with Ben between Andy and herself. Any discussions had been strictly medical—no personal observations at all. She shivered when she thought how close she'd been to making love with Andy again that last time they were together. He was just too darned attractive, and she wasn't going to test her own will-power to fend him off next time! But it hadn't stopped her thinking about him in free moments—like when she was driving the car, when she was eating, when she was sleeping…breathing…

Angrily she shook her head. Any long-term relationship would be doomed, she scolded herself: Andy's future was with his little boy in the States. She couldn't allow herself the luxury of dreaming about the two of them together in the future. She would apply herself to the matter in hand, instead of mooning over the wretched man. She would phone Veronica and ask her to come to the house instead of taking poor snuffling Amy to her.

Amy sat dolefully in her high chair, ignoring the little bowl of cereal that she usually loved, her normally bright eyes watery and puffy.

'Poor little sweetheart,' said Rosie, dropping a kiss

on the top of her hair. 'Mummy will give you something to make you feel better before Veronica comes.'

Amy's little mouth turned down and trembled ominously. 'Stay with Mummy,' she said in a croaky little voice. 'Not 'Ronica.'

Tears pricked at the back of Rosie's eyes. This was the hateful part of working, having to leave your child with someone else when she needed you—and when you didn't feel too hot yourself. I'm a real heel, she thought wretchedly. This was one of those times when she wished she were a kept woman and didn't have to go out to work. However much she loved being a GP, it would be lovely to be a stay-at-home mum just for once!

'I won't be long, Amy. And I'll bring you back a nice surprise—promise!'

But Amy wasn't in the mood to be bribed and burst into snuffly tears of distress.

Rosie took the little girl in her arms and cradled her. 'You'll be all right, darling,' she crooned soothingly, longing for nothing more than to crawl back to bed with her little girl.

The doorbell rang stridently and with a sigh Rosie put Amy back in her high chair and went to open it.

'I'm coming!' she yelled, hoping against hope it wasn't her neighbour, who had a tendency to come round at awkward times for free medical advice. If only it was someone who could come to her rescue—either a childminder or a plumber!

She flung open the door and her eyes widened in astonishment. The last person in the world she expected was standing there—Andy Templeton!

He was dressed in shorts, a loose open shirt and

trainers. He looked fit and tanned, and very, very attractive!

'What on earth are you doing here?' she gasped, her stomach doing a complete somersault at his appearance. Somehow he seemed even more devastating away from work, his open shirt revealing a tanned muscular chest that did her heart rhythm no good at all! His unexpected appearance had given her no time to put up her guard, she thought ruefully, uncomfortably aware of her tousled hair and whiter-than-white morning face.

He grinned. 'I was cleaning out the car yesterday and I found an earring—probably from our evening out at The Cascades two weeks ago.' He held out the little pearl clip, one of a pair Lily had given her. 'Thought you might have missed it, so I decided to drop it off on my way to a run on the beach.' He paused for a second and looked at her searchingly. 'I don't seem to have seen you much to talk to—except at meetings—since then.'

'No,' she said quickly. 'It's been rather a busy two weeks…'

A wail sounded behind them. Rosie looked in a harassed way behind her and then back at Andy rather apologetically. 'Thanks a lot. I'm afraid I can't ask you in. Everything's happened at once—Amy's got a virus, the washing machine's flooded and I'm supposed to be at the surgery in twenty minutes.'

Andy looked at her stressed face with an amused twinkle. 'Then I'm your man! Always available in an emergency!' He paused for a second and looked at her quizzically. 'I don't know why you didn't call on me immediately anyway. That's what colleagues—and friends—are for, surely?'

Rosie flushed rather uncomfortably. 'I didn't realise that Amy wasn't well until we got up. I thought it was a bit late to ring anyone and, of course, Ben's taken all his children sailing...'

Andy followed Rosie into the kitchen and went over to Amy, putting a gentle hand on her forehead and pursing his lips.

'Poor little girl,' he remarked. 'She does seem hot. You must stay here with her. I'll take your surgery.'

Rosie looked at him and burst out laughing. 'Dressed like that?' she said. 'I don't want to sound ungrateful, but perhaps you look just a little casual!'

'Think I might frighten the patients away? Don't worry—I've got a tracksuit in the car so I shouldn't offend the more sensitive souls. It would give you time to get a plumber...and,' he added softly, 'be with Amy. She needs you now.'

Rosie bit her lip and went across to her desolate little daughter, whose flushed cheeks had big tears rolling down them. She stroked Amy's damp hair back from her forehead. He was right—she had a choice now and, whatever her feelings about Andy, she should accept his offer. Her priority had to be Amy, and a huge flood of relief swept over her that she could look after the toddler herself.

'Thanks...thanks so much. I'd be really grateful if you would. I'll swop with one of yours next week.'

'I'd like a better reward than that,' he said softly, taking Amy out of her high chair and patting her gently on the back as she started coughing. 'When Amy's better I'd like you to come to the beach with me. We'd all enjoy a picnic, wouldn't we?'

Rosie looked at the large man holding the small child so gently and felt a lump come to her throat. This was how it could have been for Amy if she'd had a father to cherish her, someone to care about her if she was sick. It was at times like this that she felt the loneliness of widowhood more than ever...

'Yes... She would love that, Andy.' She added as an afterthought, 'And so would I.'

'Right! I'll be off, then. Hope Amy feels better soon. I prescribe plenty of TLC and a little bit of Calpol! I'll be back later to report on anything that arises in the surgery and to see this small patient!'

Cuddling Amy, Rosie watched from the door as he strode briskly down the path in his shorts, a gurgle of laughter surging up inside her at the thought of him taking surgery dressed like that. He was a man of surprises, and today she was more grateful to him than she would have thought possible. 'Now, my darling,' she whispered to Amy, 'let's see if we can't get you a little bit better before Andy gets back!' Quite suddenly, her frazzled feelings of a few minutes ago seemed to have evaporated and she felt unexpectedly light-hearted. He came just in the nick of time, she thought thankfully.

Almost guiltily she reflected that just when she'd begun to think she had her feelings for Andy under control—wham! He calls at the house and her knees go to jelly again! So much for good intentions...

She cradled Amy in her arms, and gradually the two-year-old's eyes began to droop. Rosie laid her gently on the sofa with a cushion against her side to stop her falling off, and quickly rang Veronica to tell her what had happened.

'Hopefully she'll be much better on Monday but if she isn't, could you possibly come round here?'

'No problem,' Veronica assured her. 'If you need me before then, let me know.'

She was a star, reflected Rosie, blessing the day Veronica had walked into the surgery over some minor health matter and she'd discovered that Veronica was a fully trained nursery nurse looking for work after the nursery she'd worked at had closed down.

Getting a plumber was more difficult, but after three tries she managed to get someone local who promised to come at lunchtime. She started to mop up the water that spread over the kitchen floor and put on the kettle for some tea. After all the morning's problems she still felt slightly nauseous and thirsty—perhaps drinking plenty would flush whatever she had out of her system.

She sat down with a sigh of relief beside Amy on the sofa and fell into a deep sleep.

It was the noise that woke Rosie—a stertorous, hoarse, gasping sound beside her. It took a few seconds to realise that it was Amy—her precious little girl, fighting for her breath and every few seconds giving a barking cough.

'Oh, my God!' Rosie swept the child up in her arms. 'What was I thinking of, falling asleep when you're ill?'

Consumed by guilt, she rushed into the kitchen, still holding Amy and rubbing her back gently. With one hand she put on the kettle, filled four pans with water and put them on the stove, willing them all to boil quickly and steam up the atmosphere to soothe Amy's inflamed airways.

'It's all right, sweetheart, you're going feel better very soon.' Rosie forced her voice to sound calm and controlled—just what she always advised the young mothers to do whose children had croup and had worked themselves up into a state of panic, she thought wryly.

Amy wasn't responding to her mother's soothing voice—it seemed to Rosie her breathing was getting more laboured and there was a grunting noise as she fought for each breath. Rosie suppressed the feelings of anxiety that were threatening to overtake her and paralyse her into inaction.

'Please, Amy, don't get worse, my darling.'

She opened her medical bag on the kitchen table and pulled out her stethoscope, cramming the earpieces into her ears and putting the trumpet end on Amy's chest. Listening to the whistling, wheezing sounds of Amy's lungs and the galloping heartbeat, it only confirmed her fears. She had to get Amy to hospital as soon as possible.

Her mouth dry, she rushed to the front door and, her free hand shaking, managed to open it with great difficulty. She decided it was quicker to take Amy to the local hospital herself rather than phone for an ambulance and hope it wouldn't take too long. As she ran to the garage, still holding Amy, a car drew up outside the gate, and with an overwhelming feeling of relief Rosie watched Andy step out of the car and walk towards the cottage. She rushed towards him with Amy held tightly in her arms, trying to force the words out of her dry mouth.

'Andy—quick—it's Amy. Her breathing's bad…it could be croup. I think she needs the hospital…'

He took one look at the child, summing up the situation instantly. 'Get in,' he said briskly, opening the back door of the car. 'Don't worry—we'll be there in five minutes.'

He took out his mobile phone from the glove department of his car and punched in some numbers.

'Porlstone General? Dr Templeton here—give me Fast Track Admissions. I have an infant here in acute respiratory distress—have a paediatrician and anaesthetist standing by. We'll be with you directly.'

Andy pulled away smoothly from the pavement and looked in his driving mirror at Rosie rocking Amy in her lap. He could see the distress on Rosie's face.

'Keep calm,' he said reassuringly. 'I'm sure she won't need intubating—you know it's just a sensible precaution to have everyone, including the anaesthetist, prepared.'

Rosie managed to give him a watery smile. 'Of course. It's the best thing to do…' she whispered.

Dr Miles, the paediatrician, was waiting when they arrived. Rosie hardly noticed the surroundings of the hospital and that particular antiseptic smell that seemed to hover around such places. All she was aware of was the kindly face of the plump little nurse setting up the humidified oxygen tent around Amy, and how defenceless and small her daughter seemed, lying in the cot.

Dr Miles gave a grin of recognition to Andy as they came up.

'Well, what a coincidence! Andy Templeton! It's good to see you. Last time we met you were working in Casualty here. I didn't know you'd come back to this neck of the woods.'

Andy shook his hand and turned to Rosie. 'Allow me to introduce Rosie Loveday—Amy's mum. Rosie's a colleague of mine in practice in Porlstone. Rosie, this is Gareth Miles—we were at med school together and seem to meet up from time to time!'

'I can certainly tell you're mother and daughter,' remarked Gareth Miles, giving Rosie a reassuring smile. He looked down at the distressed toddler in the cot and rubbed the trumpet end of his stethoscope in his hand to warm it.

'I'll just have a listen to Amy's chest for a second—as I'm sure you diagnosed yourself, she's probably got croup. It's quite unusual in the summer, but we have had a few cases in recently.'

He bent over the small wheezing child, gently placed the stethoscope on her chest and listened intently, moving the instrument around. Amy began to cry restlessly, her face a picture of misery, her little voice hoarse.

Gareth straightened up and stroked the baby's cheek gently. 'There, there, little one, perhaps Mum could cuddle you for a minute to calm you down.'

Rosie gathered her small daughter up in her arms and rocked her gently to and fro, her own eyes filling up with tears which she tried to blink away. Gradually Amy's cries subsided to a choking whimper and her eyes began to droop. The paediatrician watched Rosie with sympathy.

'It's not easy to be objective when it's your own child, is it?'

Rosie put Amy back in the cot and sighed, and the nurse adjusted the oxygen tent.

'I shan't ever complain about fussing parents again,' she admitted in a small voice. 'The way I've reacted to Amy being ill is a lesson to me!'

Gareth smiled. 'Don't worry too much. Her chest isn't very good at the moment, but I'm sure after a short period of oxygen it'll rapidly improve. We might also give her some nebulised adrenalin if she's not responding. Because it's viral in nature we won't give antibiotics unless there's any suggestion of a secondary infection—but I don't see any cause for too much alarm. I'll be back in about half an hour to review her. So see you both soon!'

He strode off down the ward.

'She'll soon be on the mend,' the nurse said comfortingly. 'It's amazing how soon little ones swing from one extreme to the other.' She looked perceptively at Rosie's white face and dark-circled eyes. 'Amy's asleep now. Why don't you and your husband go and have a cup of tea for a few minutes?' she suggested. 'I'll be keeping a close watch on her until Dr Miles comes back.'

Rosie felt too tired to correct her mistake regarding Andy and, close to tears, whispered, 'I can't leave her... If she should wake up....'

Andy put a comforting arm round her shoulders. 'A hot drink will do you the world of good,' he said firmly. 'We're only a minute down the corridor and the sister knows where we are.'

Rosie took a lingering glance at Amy's flushed face, and allowed herself to be led away. She looked up at Andy's strong, kind face. 'I've ruined your Saturday for you,' she sighed. 'You could have been keeping fit on the beach!'

'Don't be so darned ridiculous!' He tightened his hold on her slightly and grinned down at her. 'What kind of a monster do you think I am that I could enjoy pounding along the sands when Amy's not well?'

'I should never have fallen asleep when she was ill...'

'Nonsense—there's simply no need to feel guilty.

You probably woke up as soon as she started to wheeze—and now you know very well she's in safe hands.'

Rosie flicked a glance up at Andy—how utterly marvellous it was to have someone who understood how she was feeling to reassure her. It was so long since Tony had been around that having someone to unload her troubles to wasn't something she was used to. She'd forgotten what a very comforting feeling it was. She allowed him to shepherd her to an empty table in the canteen.

He placed a cup of steaming tea in front of Rosie, and she sipped it gratefully, smiling shakily across at him. 'I don't know how to thank you. If you hadn't arrived when you did...'

'She'll be fine—you know that better than anyone. Young children can develop high temperatures very quickly and then settle down.' He looked at her appraisingly. 'You're looking a bit peaky yourself. Have you been feeling all right?'

Rosie shrugged. 'I think I've probably caught a bit of what Amy's been incubating, but I feel much better than I did, actually—quite hungry, in fact! Probably the relief of getting Amy somewhere safe.'

He grinned at her. 'Are you so hungry you could even manage a hospital sandwich?'

Rosie looked at the next table where a large man in overalls was attacking a huge bacon buttie with great gusto. The smell had been wafting over enticingly. Suddenly an overwhelming and surprisingly ravenous feeling came over her—she longed for the salty taste of bacon encased in thick buttered bread!

'That smells pretty tempting,' she admitted longingly.

'You're every wish is my command,' Andy said, getting up and returning with two plates filled with bacon and rolls. He watched with amusement as Rosie tucked into her portion. 'You're looking better already,' he observed. 'Perhaps your blood sugar was a bit low—no breakfast, I bet.'

'I was a bit fraught this morning,' she admitted. 'Everything seemed to happen at once, and there was no one to turn to.' She started to pleat her paper serviette rather carefully and looked at him under her eyelashes. 'That was why it was such a…relief to see you, and it was very kind of you to take over my work.'

'I was glad to be of help. After all, it's what good friends are for, isn't it—to come to the rescue?'

Andy looked at her steadily, a half-smile on his lips, and Rosie felt the colour rise in her cheeks. His slight emphasis on the word 'friends' hadn't escaped her notice. If only they could be just that—friends—without the complications of that overwhelming sexual attraction she felt for him.

'You were a true friend today Andy,' she said in a low voice. 'I…I don't know what I'd have done without you, or how I can thank you enough.'

'I've told you before.' He chuckled. 'All the thanks I want is for you to let me take you both for an afternoon out. If Amy's better, how about next weekend with buckets, spades and ice cream?'

To say no would have seemed churlish, especially when she felt such gratitude to him. 'That would be lovely,' she murmured. Part of her sang at the thought, but part of her was filled with apprehension as to how she could stop her life becoming too entwined with someone whose priorities were far away.

'Then I'll keep you to it.' Andy's voice was mock-severe, but his eyes were twinkling. 'It would be nice if Lily could come, too, wouldn't it?'

'Oh, yes—that would be great! It's so kind of you.' She wondered if it was too transparently obvious that she didn't want to risk being alone with him!

His strong hand grasped hers over the table and squeezed it gently. 'Remember, Rosie,' he said with some urgency, 'friendship is a two-way thing. ''Loving friendships'' are rare—one ought to nurture them.' He was silent for a second, then he added rather bitterly, 'I'm afraid Sonia never thought of me as a friend— more as a meal ticket.'

Rosie looked at him quickly. Was that why Sonia had left him? Their eyes locked for a second and, as if reading her mind, Andy nodded sadly. 'I'm afraid we married in the first euphoria of attraction, before we got to know each other very well. When Sonia discovered my family wasn't loaded with money, she rather lost interest. I hope what we have will be deeper than that!'

Andy's eyes swept over Rosie's flushed face and tousled hair. She had such a natural look about her, he reflected. One of the lucky few who needed little make-up, with long lashes sweeping over high cheekbones and a scattering of freckles over a retroussé nose, and full sensual lips that he longed to kiss. What a contrast she was to Sonia, who had every type of beauty treatment available, was on a perpetual diet and whose main topic of conversation was money! Her only redeeming feature was that she adored Keiron, he thought grimly.

Rosie looked down at her hands, confused about what she saw in Andy's eyes. When he looked at her like that, and spoke to her in those terms, it was difficult not to believe that he felt more for her than a passing attraction. Hadn't he just said he hoped their friendship would be a 'loving' one? Perhaps after all she could allow herself to dream that she wasn't just a brief diversion and that she might, one day, be a part of his life.

Discomfited, she flicked a quick look at her watch. 'Do...do you mind if we go back? I want to be near Amy when she wakes up.'

Andy stood up abruptly. 'Of course you do. Let's get going.'

Gareth was already with Amy when they returned. He straightened up from examining her and turned to Rosie with an encouraging smile.

'Your little girl's certainly doing much better—even after so short a time her chest sounds less noisy. We'd like to keep her in for at least one night, however, and reassess her in the morning. We've got a little side ward we could put her in and a rather uncomfortable bed that you could sleep on by her side. I think you'd want to be with her, wouldn't you?'

'Oh, yes,' said Rosie gratefully. 'That would be marvellous.' She glanced at her peacefully sleeping daughter. 'If I could just slip home and collect some things while she's asleep—and leave a note for Lily so that she knows what's going on.' She gave a little giggle. 'I left a flooding washing machine and a dog in the kitchen—and I should think the plumber I requested has been and gone in disgust!'

Both men laughed and Gareth turned to Andy and punched his arm. 'So, you old reprobate—still the fittest man on the block?' He winked at Rosie. 'This guy's some athlete! At med school he was on every team we had except the ballroom formation dancing team!'

It was Rosie's turn to laugh. 'Then he should have been,' she said. 'I've seen him dance, and he's pretty good!'

She coloured suddenly. That had been the night she'd first met Andy—the night she'd let her emotions take over her senses! Neither man seemed to notice her discomfort.

'It's good to catch up with you again, Andy. You must come and see Laura, and our four little horrors.' Gareth shot a look at his watch, and looked apologetically at Rosie. 'Sorry. I've got to fly. I'll be back to look at Amy later on. In the meantime, I've promised to play cricket with my two oldest and about twenty of the neighbours' children!'

They watched him as he strode away. 'He seems a lovely man,' remarked Rosie wistfully. 'His children are so lucky to have him as a father.'

Andy chuckled. 'Couldn't have a better! I must say I admire people who have big families—I don't know how they cope! I think you and I find our single offspring enough, don't we?'

She gave a faint smile. 'You're probably right. Anyway, I must get home now and sort out the plumber and some overnight things while Amy's still asleep.'

'Let's go, then!'

By the next morning, Amy was a different child, standing up against the cot side and bouncing up and down on the mattress with gurgles of laughter.

'What a relief!' said Rosie to the nurse who had just taken Amy's temperature. 'She looked so ill yesterday. I can't believe she's her bright self again so quickly!'

The nurse smiled and stroked Amy's springy curls back from her forehead. 'She's beautiful—such lovely big brown eyes. It's really rewarding when they respond so quickly to treatment.'

Amy gave a little hiccup and then giggled, throwing herself back on the mattress with a little shriek.

'Doesn't seem much wrong with this little girl now,' remarked a deep voice behind Rosie.

Gareth was standing behind her, watching Amy with a benevolent smile. 'I'll have a quick listen to her chest, and if that sounds OK I think you can take her home.'

It was quite evident that Amy was nearly back to full and blooming health. Gareth stuffed his stethoscope back in his pocket. 'I'd keep her quiet for a day or two, but I feel no qualms about letting her go home. Is Andy taking you back?'

'No, I've got my own car with me.' She held out her hand to Gareth. 'Thank you so much for taking care of Amy for me. I can't believe she's improved so much in twenty-four hours!'

'Our pleasure.' He smiled. 'I'm glad Andy's working around here now—I'll bag him for a game of golf some time. He's a great guy.' His eyes twinkled at her. 'How wonderful that you and he have got together after the tragedy of his broken marriage to that selfish Sonia.'

Rosie opened her mouth to refute Gareth's assumption that she and Andy were an item, then closed it again as he continued earnestly, obviously under the impression that she knew about Andy's background.

'It's even worse that his little boy is so far away when Keiron is really the centre of Andy's world. I suppose he wanted Keiron to be with his mother and not suffer as he did when he was a little boy. I think he must have been very unhappy, don't you?' He paused for a second as if reflecting on his friend's life, then remarked, 'That's probably why Andy once told me he'd rather lost faith in long-term relationships—but I'm so glad he changed his mind,' he said warmly.

Rosie's heart missed a beat, and her mouth went dry—her suspicions had been right, then! Gareth had known Andy before she did and he'd know what he was talking about. She had to stop looking for a future between her and Andy.

A numbness crept through her body. Somehow the confirmation of her suspicions was too depressing to take in. Carefully she kept her face neutral. 'It does seem hard that Andy isn't near his son,' she remarked tonelessly. 'I couldn't bear to be parted from Amy.'

Gareth's words echoed in Rosie's head as she negotiated the winding bends back home, and various comments Andy had made seemed suddenly to fall into place. He'd revealed that he'd had a stepmother, and maybe that was why he was so upset that his ex-wife was getting married again. Did an unhappy childhood with a step-parent make him fear for his own child's happiness?

She unclipped Amy from her safety seat and carried her up the path, feeling a hollowness inside her. From the night they'd first met, she had allowed Andy to fill her thoughts and dreams as no other man had done since Tony had died—what a fool she'd been. Now it was blindingly obvious to her that nobody could ever be an adequate mother substitute for Keiron or restore Andy's faith in women!

'I think Andy is determined to be everything to his son,' she murmured to herself as she opened the front door. 'A stepmother for his child would never be an option.' She brushed Amy's curls back from her fore-head and added rather wistfully, 'But I wouldn't mind finding a daddy for you, darling. I think it would be a wonderful thing for both of us!'

Amy twined her arms round Rosie's neck as her mother carried her through to the kitchen. 'Yes! Find a daddy!' she shouted. 'Let Andy be the daddy! Nice Andy!'

Rosie put Amy on the floor with her bag of building bricks, and shook her head sadly. Andrew Templeton was far too committed to his own son to be anybody else's father!

CHAPTER SEVEN

'IT REALLY isn't good enough is it? Ninety-three missed appointments last month—we'll have to do something about it!' Ben looked over his glasses at Andy and Rosie. 'Any ideas?'

'What about a notice to that effect put up in the surgery? Might jolt a few people,' suggested Rosie.

The three doctors were having a quick midmorning meeting to discuss the continuing problem of patients who didn't turn up for their appointments. As Ben put it, 'A waste of money, time and resources.'

'I don't think Rosie's suggestion would be punchy enough,' remarked Andy. 'I think a letter to persistent offenders with a warning that we might not be able to treat them in the future might be more effective. I had a patient here yesterday demanding an urgent consultation when he'd just ignored his appointment the day before—and no apology or explanation!'

'It's worth trying. What do you think, Rosie?'

'I think it's a good idea. Perhaps we can reassess it in a month?'

She smiled coolly at Andy, trying to ignore the quick somersault her stomach performed when his dancing eyes met hers. Today, she said firmly to herself, was the start of her new resolution to keep her feelings for him at bay. After Gareth's revelation about Andy's troubled past, she owed it to herself and little Amy not to think of Andy as part of her future.

'Well, I'm off,' remarked Ben, lumbering out of his

chair. 'I'll see you later at the trust's meeting this lunchtime.'

Andy lifted a large armful of paper onto Rosie's desk. 'I picked these up on the way in—all your e-mail blood tests and biopsy results. I know you'll be longing to plough through them!'

Rosie nodded, not reacting to his lopsided grin, and said briskly, 'Thank you—I'll deal with them later.'

'Would a coffee help to start with?'

Rosie swallowed and closed her eyes for a second. Normally she'd be dying for a cup of restorative black coffee, but unaccountably the thought of having one at the moment made her feel distinctly queasy.

'No…not at the moment, thanks. Perhaps later on, when I've been on some visits and sorted through these tests.'

The terseness of her tone made him flick a puzzled look at her.

'Things all right, are they? Amy back to full form?'

'Yes. Absolutely fine! She seems to have forgotten completely about being ill, and trotted off very happily to Veronica's today.' There was a slight pause, then Rosie added almost reluctantly, 'I really was grateful to you the other day. It was…very kind of you to cover for me and take us to hospital.'

Andy leaned forward on the desk and looked gravely at her. 'If you're ever in trouble, Rosie, you must tell me. I'm always here for you.'

Rosie smiled faintly to herself. The truth was, he wouldn't always be there for her. He'd been a rock for her the other day, but his son would always be his first priority. It wouldn't be right to rely on Andy whenever she needed help.

'Now,' added Andy cheerily, folding his arms, 'if

you remember, you promised to come with me to the beach—you, Amy and Lily. How about the day after tomorrow? We both have half days then. The forecast is very good and I'm an expert at castle-making!'

Rosie hesitated a second. It was true, she *had* agreed to an expedition to the beach, and Amy would love it. But was it wise? More little strands to entwine him round her heart.

'Well?' he said, smiling, waiting for her answer.

'I….I don't know…' she said cautiously, 'The next few days are very busy, and I don't want to arrange something that I might have to cancel.'

His face darkened somewhat and his voice was reproachful. 'You did promise, you know. I thought you kept your promises!'

Rosie bit her lip. 'Well…perhaps, if the weather's really nice.'

He looked at her quizzically. 'You sound less than enthusiastic. You might quite enjoy it, you know!' He paused for a second, a frown creasing his brow. 'Is there something wrong, Rosie, something I should know about?'

'No…nothing's wrong. Of course we'll enjoy it…' Rosie felt contrite. Common courtesy dictated that she should fulfil her promises after his kindness to her.

'Then I'll let you get on. Speak to you later.'

He swung out of the room and Rosie stared after his retreating figure and sighed. The day ahead promised to be incredibly busy, and the last thing she wanted was bad feeling between her and Andy to worry her. After her visits there was a lunchtime meeting with the primary care trust to discuss networking the area health agencies on their computer systems. Then she had a few hours off to catch up on paperwork and check the test results that had arrived that day. Finally—and this had been weighing on her mind since the moment she'd got up—she had the most daunting part of the day to get through when she'd finished work. In an unguarded moment, she'd promised Lily that she would help out at the fashion show!

'Why on earth did I let her talk me into that?' Rosie groaned to herself. 'I must have been mad to have allowed myself to weaken, just because I felt sorry for her not having enough models!'

The charity show had assumed the proportions of a nightmare for Lily.

'Three of the models are off now for one reason or another,' she'd fretted. 'I've never had such a disaster. Normally it's one of the biggest money-raising occasions in Porlstone and now it looks like it'll be a complete non-event!'

She had looked so pathetic, her little figure hunched and her normally happy face so woebegone, that Rosie's heart had melted.

'If I can be of any help, I will...' she'd said hesitatingly.

'Oh, darling, *will* you?' Lily had exclaimed eagerly, seizing on her offer. 'You'd make the most heavenly model—especially for the evening wear, with your wonderful colouring. You'll look a princess...and, of course, the money is going towards the Porlstone Hospital renal unit, so it could help your patients!'

Rosie had opened her mouth to protest that she hadn't intended to volunteer to be a model, then she'd closed it again. She owed Lily a lot—surely she could put herself out a little for a few hours for her aunt's sake? She could only hope she wouldn't trip over going down the catwalk in one of Lily's gorgeous gowns and make a complete fool of herself!

Maria's voice came over the intercom, cutting into her thoughts. 'I've got the community nurse on the phone,' she informed Rosie. 'She'd like to speak to you urgently.'

Rosie took the call. 'Got a problem, Kay?' she asked.

'I'm at Mrs Joan Duthie's house.' The calm, no-nonsense voice of Kay Smith, the community nurse, came briskly over the phone. 'Her father, Bert Lavin, is a patient—you remember he came to stay with his daughter for a while to get his medicines sorted out? I'm on a routine visit, and I'm afraid that just before I arrived, Bert died after what was probably a sudden myocardial infarction. Could you come round and certify the death? I think Joan would be glad to see you.'

As always, when she heard of the death of a patient, Rosie felt a pang of sadness. 'I'm sorry about that, Kay, but not surprised. I'll be with you in a few minutes. I'm so glad you're with Joan at the moment.'

As she drove out of the car park, Rosie reflected that although it had been clear over the last few weeks that he was nearing the end of his life, she would miss Bert's sparky and independent personality. Of course, birth and death were part of her job, some aspects much sadder than others, and it was something that as a GP she had to get used to. But at least Bert had had a long life, and they'd enjoyed many laughs together, and the end had been mercifully quick for him. With a wry smile she recalled Andy's first day at the practice, and his insistence on accompanying her to protect her from Bert's dogs!

*   *   *

'I'm so glad it was you who came,' said Joan tearfully, as she let Rosie into the house. 'I wanted someone who'd cared for him to see him and certify his death. He was really fond of you, Dr Loveday.'

'I'm very sorry, Joan,' said Rosie, squeezing her arm comfortingly. 'He was a lovely old gentleman, and I enjoyed being his doctor. He had a grand sense of humour and endured these last few months very stoically.'

Bert was lying on the bed in the little spare room, a faded photo of his wedding day by his bed. Two army medals hung over another picture of Bert as a young man with folded arms dressed in football gear with his team.

Joan saw Rosie looking at them and smiled. 'They rather sum up my dad's life—a happy marriage, good service in the war and great times with his mates on the pitch.'

'A full life,' observed Rosie, as she bent down and put her finger on his carotid artery, listening through her stethoscope for any heartbeat. She lifted his eyelids and noted the dilated pupils and their lack of response to light.

She stood up and put her arm around Joan. 'He looks very peaceful, doesn't he? I think he would have died very quickly, and felt little pain. His failing heart was beginning to cause all kinds of problems for him.'

Joan dabbed her eyes. 'For his sake, it's a relief really,' she whispered. 'But it's awful to realise that all that generation has gone in my family—now I've no one older than me to go to for advice!'

'He'll leave a great gap for you, Joan. But you did so well, looking after him these past weeks.'

Joan smiled a watery smile. 'He was an old devil,'

she said affectionately, 'but I'm so pleased he agreed to stay with me at the end.'

She led the way into the kitchen, and Kay Smith appeared with two large cups of tea.

'Now, sit down, Joan, and get this down you,' she said firmly. 'You've had a terrible shock. Would you like me to phone your family for you—or anyone else, like a neighbour who could come and sit with you?'

Joan looked at her gratefully—someone taking charge with practical help was of great comfort.

'Perhaps you could tell my son,' she said falteringly. 'His number's on the pad. He'll come over.'

Rosie was filling in the death certificate. 'Because I've been looking after Bert and visiting him every week, I'm certain that the cause of death was his heart,' she explained gently to Joan. 'There won't be a need to inform the coroner's office in this case.'

'I'll wait till my son comes, then, and he can make all the arrangements.' Joan managed a brave smile. 'Thank you so much, Dr Loveday.'

Sad though she was about Bert's death, the sparkling beauty of the early summer morning lifted Rosie's spirits as she drove back to Porlstone. Through the fields she caught an occasional glimpse of the sea, as blue as a periwinkle, and it reminded her that in two days Andy was taking them all to the beach. Whatever she felt about being with him, Amy and Lily would love the afternoon out—she would just have to keep her own feelings in check. In time she'd get used to suppressing that lick of fire she felt every time she saw Andy. In time you could get used to anything—couldn't you?

Suddenly all thoughts of Andy were banished as a large, jagged pothole on a bend and at the side of the road took her completely by surprise. The car crashed in and out of the hole, the steering became as heavy as a steamroller's and there was an ominous flapping sound coming from the rear as the car slowly ground to a halt. Rosie gave an exasperated glance at her watch. Just when she wanted to be on time for the meeting before tackling the afternoon's work, this had to happen!

'What on earth have I done?' she muttered, scrambling out of the car and going to assess the damage at the back.

She stared in disbelief at her rear tyre, which was completely and horribly flat.

'This is where I wish I'd taken car maintenance lessons,' she groaned. 'What the hell can I do now?'

She looked wildly around. It was a very quiet road, and the only sign of life was a tractor being driven on a distant field. She would have to ring the practice and tell them what had happened and that she would probably be late for the meeting.

The line was very bad, but she managed to get the message through to Maria. However, when she rang the rescue service to come and mend the puncture, her mobile seemed to have cut out altogether.

Rosie scowled at the phone. 'Marvellous!' she growled at it, trying in vain to get some response from the numbers she punched out. Unless someone came along soon, she was stuck until she could regain communication with the outside world. There was nothing for it but to try and change the wheel herself.

She stared into the boot. She knew that she had to jack up the car first and then undo the nuts of the wheel with the spanner she'd found in a plastic bag, but the spare wheel looked dauntingly heavy. Tentatively she took out one of the instruments and looked doubtfully at it. If this was the jack, just where did one attach it? Gingerly she pushed the instrument under the rim of the car and started to lever it up with her foot. That seemed to work quite well, but getting the actual wheel off was a different matter. For minutes she tried to twist the spanner to remove the nuts but, however hard she yanked and pulled, they wouldn't yield.

'I'm going to do this if it kills me,' she muttered, so engrossed that she hardly heard the sound of a car drawing up behind her.

'You look very professional,' observed a familiar voice. 'You probably don't need my help this time!'

Rosie whirled round, her cheeks pink with effort and a small patch of oil across her nose. Her relief at seeing someone took a dive when she saw that it was Andy. She was *not* going to rely on him yet again—she had to remain at a distance, show her independence.

'It...it's OK,' she panted. 'I think I've nearly done it—just got to put the spare on now!'

He got out of his car and leaned against the door. 'So you don't need any help, then?'

'Not at all!' she said airily. To her amazement the recalcitrant nut suddenly gave, and she stumbled forward. 'There! Soon be finished!'

Andy watched her sardonically as she attempted to heave the spare wheel out of the boot. 'That's heavy, you know,' he said unnecessarily. 'Could do yourself a damage!'

She looked up at him crossly. 'OK, then, help me!' she said shortly. 'I didn't ask for you to come out, though!'

He said nothing as he manhandled the spare into position and deftly secured it into place. Then he stepped back and, wiping his hands on a rag, looked at her quizzically. 'What's biting you? I heard about your little difficulty from Maria—we both thought it better if I came and saw if I could help than leave you here for the rest of the afternoon. But perhaps that's what you wanted?'

'Of course not. I'm grateful. I…I just don't want you thinking that every time I'm in trouble you have to come running. I would have got hold of the emergency service but my mobile conked out on me.'

She sat down suddenly on the grass verge, a feeling of faintness overcoming her. It was hot, and she was very thirsty. Perhaps that was why the world seemed to be spinning round in a circle and her limbs seemed made of rubber.

'Are you OK?' There was a flicker of concern in Andy's eyes, and he bent down beside her. 'Put your head down—your BP's probably dropped slightly.'

'I…I'm fine. Nothing to worry about—just a bit hot after trying to change a wheel on one of the hottest days of the year.' Rosie shook her head at his proffered hand and forced herself upright.

Andy looked at her closely. 'Sure? Any palpitations?'

'Absolutely not! Fit as a fiddle!'

Rosie started to walk briskly back to her car and Andy frowned slightly as he watched her. He looked at his watch and said briskly, 'Then how about a long refreshing drink before the trust meeting? Like you, I'm feeling darned hot—I could do with some liquid inside me. I know we get sandwiches there but perhaps five minutes sitting in the shade would be a good idea. You look as if a break would help you, too.'

'Have we time?' asked Rosie. Suddenly the idea of a cool drink seemed irresistible—a chance to relax for a moment, even if she would be alone with Andy. Besides, she didn't want the embarrassment of feeling faint again, so perhaps sitting down for a while would revive her.

He smiled. 'We can go to my house—just four minutes away from here—and sit in the garden.'

'What about your father and aunt?'

Andy threw back his head and laughed, showing white even teeth. 'Good heavens, I'm not a teenager—they do allow me a pretty free rein now! Anyway, they've gone away for a few days with some garden society. Not that they'd mind you coming—I know they'd love to meet you. We'll leave your car here for a few minutes and go in mine.'

Rosie's heart bounded uncomfortably against her chest. It was beginning to dawn on her that her resolve to keep her feelings for Andy in check wasn't going to be easy to maintain. Sitting next to him in the car, she was only too aware of those strong, tanned hands which had once felt the most secret places of her body and aroused her senses to fever pitch. If she closed her eyes she could imagine the feel of his hard, muscular body against her, his lips invading hers with gentle persuasion. Her throat tightened at the thought, and she longed for him to take her in his arms once more... There were other reasons she wanted his company, too, she thought wistfully. His warmth, his easy manner, the fact that when she was with him she didn't feel lonely—she felt part of him.

Grow up! she said fiercely to herself. You're like a moping schoolgirl!

It was one of the most beautiful gardens Rosie had ever seen—a long lawn, bounded on either side by a colourful herbaceous border against warm golden walls, sloped down to a small cove, secluded and still. The sea could be seen through a wrought-iron gate at the garden's end, and a yacht with white sails was drifting across the water.

Rosie leant back in the reclining chair Andy had provided under an old apple tree, and lifted her face to the warm sun filtering through the branches. As she sipped the cool home-made lemonade and nibbled a biscuit, quite suddenly her vague feelings of being off colour disappeared and she felt renewed energy flowing through her. Foolishly she must have allowed herself to get dehydrated—that was probably why she'd felt so tired. She drained the rest of the glass.

Andy looked down at her with his quirky grin. 'That's obviously done you good,' he said approvingly. 'Seems to me you don't look after yourself enough! Like to see the end of the garden where we have our own little harbour?'

He held out his hand to her and pulled her out of her chair. He didn't relinquish his hold as they sauntered down the lawn towards the sea. They stood under an arch with roses and clematis twining round it just before the wrought-iron gate at the entrance to the little cove. A small rowing boat was drawn up by the rocks, and the sea rippled at the edge of the white sand.

'This is so beautiful,' breathed Rosie, entranced. 'Your own private little harbour.'

'We'll come here with Amy,' he promised. They were silent for a moment, looking out at the peaceful scene, then he took her shoulders and turned her to face him, his expression serious.

'Rosie, I'm rather puzzled—have I committed some dire wrong? I felt after we'd taken Amy to hospital that

we were getting on so well together...' His voice
dropped slightly. 'It was as if we three had known each
other for a long time...almost like a family. But today...well, your attitude towards me seems curt to say
the least. What on earth's the matter?'

His words hung in the air for a few moments and
Rosie could hear the gulls mewing overhead, the soft
swish of the waves on the shingle, smell the faint salty
smell of the sea. This was it, then. This was when she
should tell Andy that she couldn't play both parts—
that of a colleague and a girlfriend—when she knew
that there was no long-term future for them. She took
a deep breath and looked at him bravely—it was now
or never.

He gazed at her with a wistful half-smile, the wind
ruffling his thick dark hair over his forehead, his blue
eyes dancing at her. He looked impossibly handsome.
She hardened her heart.

'We have talked about this before, Andy—but now
I know more about your situation I feel it's more important than ever that we keep a certain distance between us.'

He looked quizzical. 'You think we're becoming too
close, is that it?'

Rosie's voice faltered slightly. 'You and I...well, we
did seem to have a certain rapport...'

He raised an eyebrow and said softly, 'You could
say that...right from the time we met!'

'I know—that's why this is so difficult to put into
words. You see, although we agreed to be friendly colleagues, it's not so easy when I see you so much...'

Andy frowned. 'I don't understand. Are you saying
you can't be friendly, or you're frightened you'll get
too friendly?'

Rosie drew herself up to her full height and faced him bravely. 'I'm saying that I've begun to realise that you have another life I can't be part of, Andy. And I don't want to risk Amy's and my future happiness because you can't commit yourself—and I wouldn't want you to. You aren't free to think of a future here, are you? Not with your son four thousand miles away!'

Andy stared out at the blue sparkling sea in silence. 'Perhaps,' he said at last, turning back to look down at her with an unfathomable expression in his eyes, 'I have too much baggage from my past, and I shouldn't saddle you with my worries, too...'

He started to walk slowly back up the garden beside Rosie, a feeling of despair like an icicle in his heart. He flicked a longing look at her and a sudden anger seized him. Selfish or not, he just could *not* give up on her after so many years of loneliness. After Sonia had left him, he'd doubted whether he would ever meet anyone he could fall for again. The afternoon he'd first met Rosie had been like a *coup de foudre*, love at first sight—not just her stunning looks, but her feisty attitude and her sense of fun. He clenched his fists in determination. *She* might feel it was better to cool their relationship—he was darned if he would!

'Does this mean we shan't have our afternoon on the beach?' he asked lightly.

'No, of course we'll come—I couldn't spoil Amy's and Lily's treat. I just wanted to clear the air between us, to stop anything before it got started...'

He stopped walking for a moment and looked down at her with a rough sigh. 'My sweet Rosie,' he murmured, putting an arm round her shoulders and brushing a tendril of hair away from her forehead. 'Why is life so bloody complicated?'

Their eyes locked for a moment, and Rosie felt the familiar current of attraction shudder through her. Then his arms were around her and his mouth was brushing her lips, teasing them open, fluttering over her neck, her eyes, her face.

'Let me kiss you one more time,' he murmured, holding Rosie as she attempted to break away from him. 'Just a kind of farewell?'

She looked up at him, part of her angry, part of her aware of her wild response to the feel of him against her and the longing to return his embrace. 'You mustn't do this,' she whispered. 'This isn't what I meant at all.'

'I know,' he said huskily.

His hand moved slowly over her soft body, holding her full breasts, following the line of her waist and her legs. Rosie felt her resolve slip further and further away. Her arms crept round his neck, and suddenly she was returning his kisses. Their mouths meshed and they explored each other hungrily, her body arching against his, feeling his urgent need for her, the flood of ardour making her tremble.

The sound of Andy's mobile phone was like a thunderbolt. Momentarily they stared at each other, dazed and still shaken by the intensity of their passion. Andy pulled the phone out of his pocket and stepped back from her, his tousled hair ruffling his forehead, his eyes still holding hers.

'Remember, I hadn't quite finished our farewell.' He grinned, his eyes dancing. He answered the mobile. 'Yes? Andy Templeton here. Right, I'll be there. Er…yes, I think I can get hold of Rosie Loveday. I'll pass the message on!'

Andy snapped shut the mobile and put it back in his pocket. 'They want me to find you and tell you the meeting's going to start ten minutes earlier. Perhaps we'd better go!'

He took her hand and they ran back up the lawn to the car.

'Darling, you look absolutely wonderful!' Lily stepped back from Rosie and gazed at her with her head cocked to one side.

'I don't think I do justice to this lovely dress,' protested Rosie.

She looked doubtfully at her pale reflection in the long mirror. No wonder she was pale. After the day she'd had, she felt rather like a wet rag—her emotions as jangled as if they'd been in a mixer! Just where did she stand with Andy now? she wondered. So much for her firm resolve to cool things down between them!

'Believe me,' Lily assured her, 'that tangerine taffeta gives you a lovely golden glow—don't you agree, girls?'

Amidst the organised chaos of the fashion show, the other models all chorused their agreement. Rosie stood in their midst, wearing a tight, backless, long dress which enhanced her small waist, the deep colour of the material contrasting beautifully with the honey colour of her hair. A worried assistant of Lily's was rushing round with pins in her mouth, making small adjustments to everyone's dresses.

'It feels a little tight,' Rosie murmured, an avalanche of panic overcoming her at the thought of making her way down the catwalk in a few minutes. 'I hope it won't split as I make my entrance!'

'You'll be so, so good!' promised Lily. 'All your clothes are here on the stand in the order you wear them, and Arabelle here will be your dresser. I'm going out front now to announce everything.' She cast a professional look round her team of models. 'Good luck, everyone!'

Rosie looked at the woman who was going to help her get into each outfit with surprise. 'Why, Arabelle! I didn't know you were involved in this!'

Arabelle smiled back at her. 'Dr Loveday! I didn't know you were involved either!'

'I'm just helping my Aunt Lily out.' Rosie chuckled. 'I'm no model, but she had some problems organising it this year—and do call me Rosie!' She looked appraisingly at Arabelle. 'You look really well—have you been somewhere exciting?'

'Yes, we've just had a holiday in Florida, partly business. I'm helping because my husband knows Lily—he's in the fashion business, and she's a very good customer.'

'Come on!' whispered a voice. 'Rosie, you're on now!'

Hastily Rosie sallied onto the catwalk, thankful that she was wearing a long dress that wouldn't show her knocking knees, trying to swing her walk to the timing of the music. Arabelle was waiting for her when she got back, ready to tear off the long evening dress and help Rosie into a smart cream trouser suit.

'Tell me,' whispered Rosie as her hair was brushed for her and buttons done up, 'Have you had a word with your husband about—?'

'Having babies?' finished Arabelle for her with a rather sad smile. 'Yes. I took my courage in both hands and told him everything. I can't say he was over the moon, but he was really concerned about the fibroids— more than I thought he would be, really. I got the feeling he *might* be persuaded to be a father again!

Actually,' she added, 'he should be here tonight but we only got back yesterday, and he's feeling a bit under the weather—probably jet lag. I told him to stay in bed.'

'It does sound as if he's not entirely against the idea, then,' said Rosie, smiling. 'And at least he knows how you feel.' She got ready to do her next stint on the catwalk.

The evening seemed to be a triumph. Lily was ecstatic, her little figure flitting everywhere, congratulating all her helpers and opening bottles of champagne to celebrate raising yet more money for a good cause. There were delicious little canapés and tiny smoked salmon sandwiches. Rosie felt ravenous after the strain of the evening—which she found to her surprise she'd actually enjoyed—and took several. Everyone seemed very relaxed and there were a few short speeches. Rosie leant against the wall and listened to them, watching Lily fondly and thinking how marvellous she looked in a glittering black sheath dress and long drop pearl earrings.

The urge to be horribly and violently sick came over her without warning. With a terrific effort she managed to edge her way through the crowds and scramble to the ladies in time and without anyone noticing her. She sat for a while on a stool after she'd got rid of the sandwiches she'd just eaten so heartily and stared at herself in the mirror for a minute. Then she got up and took out her medical bag from a locker by the basin and reached into it. With a feeling of inexorable certainty she knew what was wrong with her, and it wouldn't take long to find out.

A few minutes later she stared at the phial in her

hand, holding it up to the light, then she looked at her pale reflection again.

'There's no doubt about it, Rosie Loveday,' she whispered slowly. 'You're absolutely and undoubtedly pregnant!'

CHAPTER EIGHT

ROSIE sipped the tea she was having with Maria before the morning's surgery, and stared unseeingly at the photographs Maria was showing her of her latest boy-friend. She hardly took in the interesting details of the row Maria had had with the boy's parents or the plans she was making for their engagement party. Instead, a recurring question sounded over and over in her mind, like rewinding a tape—after just one intimate encounter with Andy—and him a doctor, for heaven's sake—how could she be having his baby? Then she smiled wryly to herself. It seemed to happen to her patients often enough!

Of course, one day she'd hoped, in the right circum-stances, to have a brother or sister for Amy—she had always regretted being an only child herself—but *now,* when she'd just started a new job in a new location, and without the security of knowing that she and Andy would be together for ever? She could hardly believe the evidence of the numerous pregnancy tests she'd done over the past two days, and as her cycle tended to be chaotic normally, she hadn't worried when she'd missed two periods. She shook her head despairingly—it was too complicated to think about. She had to apply herself to the problems the day would bring.

'So, you see, I'm not asking Dave's mum and dad—they can go whistle in the wind. Don't you think I'm right?'

Through her fog of worried thoughts, Rosie suddenly

143

became aware that Maria was waiting for some reaction from her.

'What?... Yes, yes, of course you're right, Maria. Better to leave them well alone.'

Satisfied, Maria went to answer the phone, and Rosie looked numbly at the posters on the surgery wall—so many of them to do with babies, their immunisations, when they should go for check-ups and when the antenatal clinics were held. She bit her lip. Soon she would have to plunge herself into that life again. And just how was she going to manage and, more dauntingly, just how was she going to tell Andy that he was about to be a father again? That afternoon he was taking Amy, Lily and herself to the beach—hardly the time to blurt out that she was having his child, yet it was something she couldn't keep a secret for long.

Easier said than done, she thought ruefully as she sat down at her desk. She just couldn't block out the mixture of emotions that were whirling round in her head—part fear, part incredulity but mostly a feeling of excited anticipation!

It was ironic that her first patient should be a very new baby. Rosie looked at little Lucy Bradwell with special interest, thinking that in seven months' time she, too, would have a baby like Lucy—with all the demands a tiny child made. Lucy had arrived almost four weeks early and was only three weeks old now, with a mop of black hair and a complexion like a rose petal. Rosie took her in her arms and cradled her tenderly.

'She's so beautiful,' she remarked softly. 'She looks as if she's doing very well. Is she keeping you up at night?'

Karen, Lucy's mother, was very young and looked

pale and exhausted. She gave a watery smile and then two tears rolled down her cheeks. 'I didn't know it would be like this.' She sniffed miserably. 'I'm so tired, and the baby just seems to scream all the time. Even when I feed her, she's still not satisfied. She draws her little legs up as if she's in pain. I don't think I'm very good at looking after babies!'

Rosie gave Karen a reassuring smile. 'Of course you are! I see from the midwife's notes that her weight's very good—remember, her system's less mature than that of a full-term baby. She may be slightly constipated and colicky but, honestly, she looks very well to me. You're doing so well, feeding her yourself. I promise you in a week or two she'll be that much bigger, able to take more milk and will probably sleep a little longer.'

Karen groaned. 'Seems a long time to wait!'

Rosie laid the baby on a blanket on the examination couch, felt her tummy and listened to her bowel sounds.

'I can't hear anything untoward, and I think it's just the slight immaturity of her bowel that's causing her discomfort. Normally breastfed babies don't suffer from constipation. I'd like you to try her with some cool boiled water between feeds—that may just help a little. Can anyone take her for an hour or two in the day so you can have a nap?'

'Mum says she'll come over. The trouble is that Dave's on night shift and he sleeps during the day, so I don't want him to hear Lucy.' She sighed. 'She seems to take up every minute of the day—I don't get anything else done at all. I do love her, but it makes you wonder why people have babies—it's never-ending, isn't it?'

Karen's words hung in the air as she departed with her baby daughter, and Rosie bit her lip. The days after she'd had Amy came back to her with clarity. It had been a bitter-sweet time—her joy at having her beautiful little daughter had been so clouded by her thoughts of Tony and the fact that when other fathers had come to the hospital to visit their babies there had been no one for her. Of course darling Lily and her uncle had come up to help her—but it hadn't been quite the same.

And now she had another baby on the way, unplanned and by a father who might be devastated by the news. Rosie picked up a pencil and began doodling absently on her pad. Some would say she'd been an irresponsible fool. But, she thought fiercely, she would never forget that night of passion and rapture with Andy. In some way it had released her from the chains of grief she'd felt so long for Tony. She didn't regret it, not even now when she was reaping the consequences. A dart of excitement and determination flickered through her. This baby would be loved and adored, just as Amy was!

For the next hour Rosie pushed her personal circumstances to the back of her mind and concentrated on the usual diversity of patients who wended their way through her surgery. The last patient had been fitted in as an emergency, and Rosie was interested to see that it was Arabelle Carter's husband—she remembered Andy had said they lived near his house and that Mr Carter seemed a rather bombastic individual.

Arabelle came in, supporting her husband. He was a well set-up older man with thick white hair, distinguished-looking and with an air of authority. As he entered the room he looked pale and was evidently having trouble even walking to the chair that Rosie pushed towards him.

'This isn't my idea,' he said aggressively as he sat down with a grimace. 'I can't stand all this fuss, fuss, fuss! I've obviously got a strained muscle or something...'

'But he seems in agony at night,' said Arabelle anxiously. 'And his leg looks very strange to me—huge and puffy.' She made an attempt at a weak joke. 'You'd think when you'd just had a holiday you'd be raring to go!'

'Ah, yes, you've just been to Florida, haven't you?' said Rosie, remembering the conversation she'd had with Arabelle at the fashion show. 'I think I'd better take a look at your leg. Do you remember twisting or injuring it in any way in the last week?'

Justin Carter lay on the examination couch and scowled. 'I felt as fit as a fiddle until the day after we landed. Meant to go to that fashion show but my leg really began to give me trouble so Arabelle wouldn't let me go. First time she's got her own way,' he commented dryly.

Rosie looked at her patient's leg silently. The whole leg was severely swollen and red. Compared to his other leg, it looked elephantine. She felt it gently and the man winced with a sharp intake of breath. Alarm bells rang in her head.

'This doesn't look too good,' she said gravely. 'To be on the safe side, I think you ought to go to hospital. I'd like you to see a consultant.'

Justin shook his head irritably. 'And what could he do that you can't? I'm a busy man, Doctor. Surely a few painkillers would do the trick?'

Rosie shook her head. 'I suspect you might have a

deep vein thrombosis which, with that amount of swelling, going right up the thigh, is likely to be in the iliac vein. It's the kind of thing that can occur on a long flight when you're relatively immobile.'

'Is that bad, Rosie?' asked Arabella, looking rather dazed.

'Your husband needs anticoagulant drugs which could be injected into the vein to break up the clot. If he doesn't have them, the clot could impede the blood flow in the leg—as you can see, I think it's already restricted.'

'I can't possibly go to hospital,' growled Justin, struggling to sit up on the couch. 'I have hundreds of orders to process, and I'm due in London in two days' time. I can't believe it's so serious I've got to be hospitalised.'

Rosie was already lifting the phone. 'I'm ringing for an ambulance, Mr Carter. I don't want to be alarmist, but I don't want to risk you having a pulmonary embolism. You're to move that leg as little as possible.'

'This is ridiculous,' muttered the man. 'I've never had anything like this before—are you sure?'

'Ninety-nine per cent sure. You've just been immobile for quite a few hours, and I see from your notes that you're a smoker. Did you walk around during the flight?'

'No,' he admitted. 'I was asleep for most of the journey.'

'Then let's not take any chances. There are a number of tests they'll do to check the diagnosis.'

For the first time Justin started to look a little uneasy. 'What kind of tests?' he muttered.

'A thrombosis can be diagnosed by venography, in

which a dye is introduced into the vein and an X-ray taken. Or they may use Doppler ultrasound scanning.'

Husband and wife stared at each other as Rosie ordered the ambulance, then suddenly Justin heaved himself upright and said churlishly. 'For God's sake, can't you give me aspirin or something—doesn't that disperse clots?'

'I think you're going to need something stronger than that.'

He stared mulishly at her. 'Look, I want to see another doctor—get another opinion! I've got a million-pound order on my books that I've got to oversee. If I lose it, my business may go down the tube!'

Rosie sighed. Sometimes patients who made a fuss about not having treatment were more of a nuisance than those who constantly demanded attention! She spoke over the intercom to Maria.

'Could you send either Dr Cummings or Dr Templeton in for a second when they can, Maria? I'd like another opinion on a patient I have here.'

Two minutes later Andy walked in and looked enquiringly at Rosie. 'You wanted to see me?'

'I want another opinion,' growled Justin Carter. 'I like to be sure about things when I take advice. I've nothing against Dr Loveday, but I'm not going to hospital if it's not necessary!'

Andy didn't comment but listened to what Rosie told him then examined the leg carefully. He had an air of quiet authority, reflected Rosie, that seemed to subdue Justin's aggressive attitude—or perhaps, she thought cynically, it was because he had more confidence in male doctors!

Andy looked at the patient. 'I completely agree with Dr Loveday,' he said quietly. 'It's very possible that you have a DVT—deep vein thrombosis. For an accurate diagnosis you should be in hospital.'

Justin gave a long-suffering sigh. 'You doctors, you all stick together. Who's going to run my business for me?'

Andy folded his arms and looked down at the man kindly. Perhaps he realised that part of the patient's bluster was born of fear and a need to feel in control of the situation.

'Mr Carter,' he said gently, 'I don't think you really feel up to running your business anyway at the moment, if you're honest. Surely you have someone who can carry on for you?' He looked up at Arabelle enquiringly.

'Of course he has,' exclaimed Arabelle. 'I know all about the business. After all, that's how I met him—I was his PA!'

'Problem solved, then,' said Andy, smiling. 'I'm sure you'd rather be safe than sorry!'

Justin turned to Rosie and muttered reluctantly, 'Very well, then—I'll go if I have to.'

'Thanks a lot,' said Rosie to Andy when her patient had been carried out by the paramedics. 'He was hard to persuade. He must be hell to live with—more stubborn than an ox! You worked wonders!'

Andy grinned. 'My natural charm,' he said modestly. He started to leave the room, then turned at the door. 'I'll pick you up at two o'clock to go to the beach—I'm looking forward to it. Looks like it's going to be a perfect afternoon for us all to relax and enjoy ourselves.'

'Yes,' said Rosie hollowly. She glanced at his smiling face and her throat constricted. It was going to be a strange afternoon, that was for sure. She doubted if she'd be able to relax, trying to decide just if or when she should reveal her pregnancy to Andy!

It *was* a perfect afternoon, reflected Rosie as she looked at her little daughter energetically digging a hole in the sand and watching the waves run into it. The sun was dazzling and, although they were in a secluded little cove, the tide had gone out enough for them to see plenty of other families enjoying the summer afternoon. Shrieks of laughter and the click of bat on ball wafted over to them.

Lily, who'd come in her own car from the shop, wore a large straw hat and smart white trousers and was lying back in a sunchair with a glass of wine in her hand. She and Amy kept up a running dialogue as Amy ran backwards and forwards from the sea's edge with little presents for her of shells, stones and even a pail of sea water.

'Amy, darling, you're spoiling me—all these lovely things from the seashore! I shall put them in the sandwich box when we've eaten our tea!'

Amy looked pleased. 'Tea and cakes!' she said with great satisfaction, then added hopefully, 'Now?'

'Uh, not yet, sweetheart. Before tea we have to go for a swim,' said Andy firmly, squatting down on the sand beside the little girl. He held his hand out to her. 'Don't you want to feel what it's like to splash in the sea with me?'

Rosie watched the two figures running off towards the water, Amy's chubby little figure a sweet contrast to Andy's tall, muscular body, set off to advantage by his swimming trunks. He looked a perfect father as he held the giggling child his arms and swung her up and down in the waves. Just how would he react if she was to reveal she was to have his child? Would he be pleased, horrified, stunned? Worse, she thought gloomily, would he feel she was trying to trap him into a permanent relationship?

They were running back to her again, and Amy flung her wet little body on Rosie.

'You come, too, Mummy!' She tugged at Rosie's arm. 'Andy push you in the waves!'

'Good idea!' Andy looked down at Rosie, his eyes sweeping over her slender, bikini-clad body lying back on the rug. 'Work up an appetite!'

He bent down and pulled her up by her hand and she groaned, 'Have I got to?'

'Yes!' shouted Amy enthusiastically.

Then they each took Amy by the hand and ran with her to the water's edge. Lily watched them through narrowed eyes, and a little knowing smile played round her lips as she had another sip of wine.

The afternoon was a huge success—especially from Amy's point of view. She loved everything—jumping in and out of the waves, running with Boggle along the sands and standing watching the cricketers on the next beach. Eventually she sat on Lily's knee whilst Lily read her a story, and her eyes began to droop. Lily stood up with Amy in her arms.

'I'm going to pop home with this little girl now,' she said. 'I've got some paperwork on the shop to do. It's been absolutely lovely here, but I think we're both tired now, aren't we, poppet?'

Rosie looked at her, startled, and her stomach took a swift dive. She couldn't be left alone with Andy now! She wasn't ready to tell him her news—she wasn't even sure she *could* tell him.

'I'll come with you, Auntie,' she said quickly. 'It's time we all made a move anyway.'

Lily looked at her imperiously. 'You stay and get the afternoon sun,' she said firmly, 'And you can bring all the picnic stuff and chairs with you later. Amy and I want to go off together, don't we, my lamb?'

Rosie watched them disappear up Andy's garden and back to the road, then turned slowly back to where Andy was sitting, throwing sticks for the dog. He looked up and smiled at her, that lazy familiar smile that made her heart turn over. He patted the rug beside him.

'Come and sit here,' he said. 'I think Amy and your aunt would give the afternoon ten out of ten, don't you?'

'You were very good with Amy.' She nearly added, You're like the father she never had, but bit the words back.

'The feeling was mutual.'

Rosie looked at him under her lashes. 'You…you like children, don't you?'

'Of course—especially children like Amy. She's full of life.'

'I expect your son is lively, too.' She started to rub suntan lotion onto her arms. 'Did you ever wish you'd had more than one child?' she asked casually.

Andy laughed. 'He's a cheeky handful—one of him is more than enough for me. He would have loved it here this afternoon, enjoyed showing Amy all his favourite haunts.'

Rosie let handfuls of sand sift through her fingers into a little pile on the ground. 'It…it seems unfair that he should be so far away from you. Surely you could have got a court order for him to stay in this country while he was growing up?'

Andy was silent for a second, then he sighed. 'When I was a little boy, Rosie, my parents split up. My mother ran away with her lover and my father refused to let me see her. There were numerous court cases, and I felt like a little pawn in the middle. It was as if I were an instrument by which my parents could hurt each other.'

'So who did you live with in the end?'

There was a trace of bitterness in his voice. 'My father and stepmother. I very rarely saw my mother, and there were terrible rows between my parents when I was taken to see her. The atmosphere was very nasty.'

Rosie looked at him in horror. 'What a cruel thing to do to a child,' she whispered. 'You must have been very unhappy.'

He nodded. 'I believed that I was unloved, unwanted, a little parcel of humanity with no feelings—to be shoved around.' His wonderful clear blue eyes held hers for a moment. 'That's why, you see, I'd rather Keiron saw his parents as friends, even if Sonia and I are no longer married. I'm determined to do what's best for my son, to let him feel he's loved very much by both of us. I never thought I was anyone's priority—and it hurt.'

Rosie was silent and her heart ached for the man. He had been so hurt and bruised by his childhood, no wonder he was determined not to let history repeat itself. But where does it leave me and my baby? she thought sadly. It was obvious that another child would upset his already complicated life, and fragments of conversation they'd had floated back to her when he'd given the impression that one child was enough for him. There was never going to be an easy way or time to tell Andy.

In an agony of indecision she rolled over on her stomach and watched a little yacht tacking its way across the bay. Perhaps, she thought miserably, she should move away again—go back North and have the baby there! Problems whirled round in her head like so many ingredients in a mixer.

'You seem deep in thought.' Andy's deep voice interrupted her worried thoughts. 'What are you dreaming about?'

Rosie sat up abruptly. 'Oh, nothing much—just things I have to plan for...'

He put his arm round her shoulders. 'I've been thinking of plans myself,' he commented lightly. 'I might bring Keiron back over here for the summer—that is, if he wanted to.'

And if he didn't want to? Rosie smiled inwardly. Of course Andy would do what his son wanted. She wondered curiously what this little boy was like. Undoubtedly well loved, but nevertheless having to cope with parents far apart—it was a strange situation.

'Would you ever move to the States to be near him?' she asked. 'I know you didn't initially go there because you were still taking exams here.'

He nodded and sighed. 'Of course—if I could get the right job near Keiron, I can see that happening.'

Rosie was silent. Then what future could there be between them? She could never agree to move there. Home was the country of her birth, where Lily was, and Amy was happy. How complicated life would get if he knew she was having his child!

She began to gather their things together. 'Time to

go,' she said firmly, slipping on a pair of shorts and a T-shirt over her bikini.

As they walked back to the car together, Andy looked down at her with his heart-melting smile and took her hand, pulling her towards him gently and brushing her hair from her forehead. 'What a lovely, happy afternoon we all had together,' he murmured.

Rosie stiffened, her heart starting to gallop at his touch, as if a switch had turned on an electric current between them. 'We must go, Andy,' she said breathlessly. 'It's getting a bit late…'

His eyes danced at her. 'We never finished what we started yesterday,' he murmured. 'Remember? We were just in the middle of saying farewell to each other in the garden, like this, when we were rudely interrupted by the phone!'

He drew her towards him and, looking deep into her eyes, held her face in his hands and brushed her mouth with his. Then his kiss became harder, more passionate and she felt the inevitable response of her body and the familiar liquid feeling of desire flooding through her. His hands started to stray over her wantonly, her breasts, her waist and back, and every erogenous zone in her body cried out for him to make love to her.

With hard and desperate determination she pushed him away—this was utterly ridiculous. She couldn't allow him to do this when she didn't even know if she could tell him about their baby!

'Please, Andy…that's enough of the farewells,' she said shakily. 'I…I need to get back and help Lily put Amy to bed.' She turned away from him and started walking up the garden—she didn't want him to see the longing in her eyes.

He took the picnic basket from her and murmured,

'Whatever you say, sweetheart.' His glance swept over her appraisingly. 'I think the afternoon's done you good—there's more colour in your cheeks. I told you it would be an opportunity to relax!'

Rosie sighed—the truth was, she couldn't remember ever feeling so churned up in her life!

CHAPTER NINE

THE ringing of Rosie's phone was insistent and loud. It was impossible to ignore it even if one was cosily asleep and in the middle of a lovely dream—a dream that entailed her walking with Andy, pushing a pram with a smiling baby lying in it, and Boggle and Amy running ahead down to the sea.

She turned over and groaned, wondering through the fog of sleep why anyone should phone her at two o'clock in the morning when she wasn't on call. Then the cold hand of reality gripped her heart, and brought her back to the bleak truth that she hadn't yet made up her mind whether to tell Andy or not about her pregnancy.

'Yes?' she croaked.

A familiar deep voice sounded in her ear. 'Rosie, sorry to disturb you, but we need your help.'

Suddenly wide awake, she sat up abruptly. 'Andy? What's happened?'

His voice was clipped. 'There's been an RTA on the old country road—a bus carrying a lot of holiday-makers smashed into a sports car and has rolled part way down the cliff. We need everyone we can get at the hospital.'

'Sure. I'm on my way.'

It had to be a major incident to call in all the local doctors. It didn't take long to scramble into some clothes and whisper to a bemused Lily where she was going, before driving as fast as she dared to Porlstone

General Hospital, all thoughts of her pregnancy pushed
well to the background. She felt the familiar dry mouth
and quickened heartbeat which, when she'd been a junior hospital doctor, had always kicked in when something major had happened.

The emergency department was lit up, the driveway
littered with ambulances, blue lights still flashing.
Rosie could see Andy in a white coat at the entrance,
a clipboard in his hand, making notes as each patient
was stretchered in, some already attached to drips.

'Go through to the small ops theatre—Sister's there
and she's organising things,' said Andy as Rosie ran
up. He motioned to a crowded reception area with people lying on trolleys, rather like a battle area. 'It's
pretty grim—two people in ICU.'

Rosie took a sharp breath. The patients seemed to be
mostly elderly, some of them completely stunned, others bravely trying to comfort their friends.

Sister Betty O'Connor seemed like an oasis of calm
amidst the frenzied activity of trolleys being pushed
into side cubicles and porters bringing wheelchairs and
oxygen cylinders into the main corridor. Staff brought
in from other wards mingled with policemen standing,
grim-faced, waiting to interview the walking injured.

'Thanks for coming—I'm so glad Andy got hold of
you. Perhaps you'd better put this on,' she said, handing Rosie a white coat. 'Then can you cross-match the
bloods of the man in the next cubicle and do his obs?
He's the driver of the car involved—he's in shock, as
you might guess. He's just been wheeled in.'

Rosie flicked a quick look at the patient's name on
the chart at the end of the trolley. He wasn't very old—
possibly in his late thirties. A large gash stood out liv-
idly red on his forehead, and a huge area of his chest

was already turning mottled blue and purple. She attached a sensor on his arm to the Dynamap machine, which gave a constant reading of his blood pressure, and prepared to draw off some blood.

'Mr Hawkstone,' she said softly but clearly, noting the man's pallid complexion and grey lips. 'I'm just checking your blood pressure…'

He looked nervously at her. 'And what are you doing with that needle?'

'Taking some blood so that we'll know your blood group and can match it up if you need a transfusion.'

The man struggled feebly to get up. 'Don't do that… I don't want it done!'

'It won't hurt in the least,' soothed Rosie reassuringly. 'Please, lie back—it'll be very quick.'

She bent over the man's arm and pinched his skin to show up a vein. Just as she was about to insert the needle he jerked his arm away, and with a sudden surge of energy punched his other arm towards her. With a lightning-fast reaction Rosie dodged his punch, but staggered back with a crash against a cupboard.

'I told you I don't want you to do that,' he muttered in a slightly slurred way.

'For goodness' sake,' yelped Rosie, as the needle hurtled across the bed, narrowly missing her face. 'What do you think you're doing?'

The curtain swished open just as Rosie was recovering her balance, and Andy came in. 'What's all the noise about?' he asked, looking sharply at Rosie.

She shrugged. 'Mr Hawkstone,' she said coldly, 'seems reluctant to let me take any of his blood.'

Andy raised one brow and said grimly. 'Really? I wonder why that is.'

He bent over the torpid figure of the man for a second, then turned back to Rosie, pulling a face. He dropped his voice. 'Could be he's unwilling because he's been drinking. You obviously haven't got near enough yet to smell his breath—it reeks of alcohol.'

He turned to squint at the Dynamap gauge. 'BP's a bit low—85 over 50. I'll get some Haemacell into him.'

He hooked up a bag of the replacement fluid, which would counteract the effects of shock, and watched as Rosie bent over Mr Hawkstone, listening to his chest through her stethoscope. Her face was expressionless as she looked up at Andy. 'Sounds a bit laboured— how soon can he go for X-ray?'

'There's a bit of a backlog, I think. He might be haemorraging somewhere so I'll try and get a portable X-ray unit in.'

The man stirred fretfully. 'It wasn't my fault,' he whispered hoarsely. 'I didn't expect to see a bloody bus on the road at that time of night.'

Rosie's eyes met Andy's—it wasn't up to them to apportion blame, but a cold feeling of fury was beginning to creep through Rosie's soul. Three years ago a drunken driver had killed her husband and Amy's father. Many people had been affected by Tony's death— she couldn't help her bitter thoughts as she hooked an oxygen mask over Edward Hawkstone's face and adjusted his drip. Every time she dealt with the results of a drunk-driving accident it brought back memories of that terrible night. It was hard to keep a detached frame of mind in such circumstances.

Betty O'Connor bustled in. 'How's Mr Hawkstone?'

'We need an X-ray p.d.q. Can you speed things up?'

'I'll do my best,' she said dryly, swishing back through the curtains again. A few moments later she reappeared. 'I've Mr Hawkstone's wife here.' she said in a low voice. 'Is he OK to see her?'

Rosie nodded. 'That'll be fine.'

An attractive blonde woman came in, her faced tearstained and scared. She stared wordlessly at her husband, overawed by the sight of him hooked up to drips and the terrible bruising on his chest.

'Heavens, Edward, what on earth have you done to yourself?' she breathed at last.

Andy pushed a chair forward and gently sat her down. 'Don't worry about all the tubes.' He smiled kindly at her. 'We're just waiting for him to go to X-Ray—we'll have a better picture of any injuries he has then.'

Mrs Hawkstone nodded wordlessly, still staring at her husband's face, then she took his hand in hers and clutched it tightly. 'How…how did it happen?' she whispered. 'I was so worried when you were late back from the dinner…'

Edward Hawkstone grimaced. 'These buses…they're too damn large for country lanes. I tried to avoid it, but…' His voice faded and his head flopped back on the pillow as he stared at the ceiling.

'They're ready for Mr Hawkstone in X-Ray.' A porter appeared by the curtains and Andy helped him manoeuvre the trolley into the corridor. Mrs Hawkstone looked at both doctors uncertainly. 'He…he'll be all right, won't he?' she asked tremulously.

'Yes. Don't worry,' said Rosie. 'He'll be fine.'

She wondered if the people in ICU would be all right, then sighed. For all she knew, the bus might have been on the wrong side of the road but, as sure as anything, Edward Hawkstone's reactions would have been seriously compromised by his alcohol level.

'Perhaps you'd like to go and get some tea, Mrs Hawkstone? Your husband may be some time—and I'm sure, whatever they find when they X-ray him, he'll have to stay in for observation at least. I think Sister's ringing around now. We'll let you know.'

Mrs Hawkstone trailed off dejectedly down the corridor and Rosie stared after her. Who knew how that woman's life would change after the events of tonight? And all because her husband had had too much to drink.

It was a long and grim night. One of the passengers from the bus collapsed and died from a heart attack despite all the staff's best efforts, and a patient in ICU had her leg amputated. Her eyes gritty with sleep, Rosie slumped down in the small kitchen off Casualty and put her head in her arms. She hadn't dealt with this sort of situation for a few years and she'd forgotten how emotionally draining it could be.

Betty came in and poured herself a large black coffee, then waved the jug at Rosie.

'Will you have one?' she asked. 'It's been a pretty fraught night, I'm afraid.' She paused for a second, then said brusquely, 'The bus driver's only got a slim chance—they're moving him to the neuro unit at St Catherine's.'

Rosie looked at her steadily. 'You know the driver of the car was reeking of drink, don't you?'

Betty got up with a sigh from the chair she'd collapsed into a minute before. 'The police will get all the facts,' she said gently, then pulled a wry face. 'No matter how long I'm in this job, I don't seem to get used to these tragedies—so bloody unnecessary, some of them.'

She trudged out and Rosie glanced at her watch.

Four o'clock! No wonder she felt like a zombie. She got up and stretched, then heard sounds of quiet crying outside in the corridor. She went to the door and saw a young nurse helping an elderly woman to the private room that was used by bereaved relatives. Andy was walking behind them.

'What happened?' Rosie asked him softly.

He looked grim. 'I just had to tell her that her husband has died—multiple internal injuries. They were on a holiday to celebrate their golden wedding anniversary.'

Rosie's eyes filled with tears. 'Poor things—they didn't deserve that.'

Andy looked at her perceptively, then took her arm and led her back into the kitchen. 'This has really got to you, hasn't it?'

Rosie put her hands up to her face. 'I'm sorry. It's just…just that it brings back to me the night that Tony died. I know how that poor woman is feeling. The drunk who mowed Tony down had the same excuse as that man made tonight. He said it wasn't his fault—he said that Tony must have walked into the path of his car. I saw Tony's body, and I shall never forget it. The man must have been racing like a lunatic out of that car park to inflict the damage he did.'

She looked at him bleakly and Andy put his arms round her and rocked her against him, as one would to soothe a child.

'You poor sweetheart,' he murmured. 'What a pity you had to deal with that man tonight.'

How comforting his warm body was! She could feel the steady beat of his heart against hers, the strength of his embrace calming her, restoring her equilibrium. Then astoundingly and without warning a wonderful feeling of peace stole over her and she realised with blinding clarity that the grief she'd felt for Tony had finally disappeared. Yes, the night had brought back memories of the terrible evening of his death, but it was as if she were remembering someone she'd known a long, long time ago, in another life. Now someone else had taken the place of that emptiness. That was something she'd known for a long time really—an overwhelming love for the man who was holding her so close to him at that moment. It was odd that the blinding flash of insight she'd just had should come after a night of tragedy.

She relaxed thankfully against Andy, allowing this new-found serenity to lap over her. At last she realised she could put her grief for Tony finally behind her, allow herself to love and live again without any guilt. She leant her head against Andy's face for a moment, the morning stubble of his chin scratching her cheek. He'd been up longer than she had—he must be exhausted, too. She pulled gently away from him and smiled at him.

'I've got to learn to overcome these things. It's all part of the job, isn't it?'

'It doesn't make it any easier, though,' he said gently, then added, 'You must be dropping on your feet. Shall I drive you home?'

Again a feeling of love for him swept through her—he was so sweet and kind. Was she doing the right thing to keep her pregnancy from him, even if his future was in the States? It was a dilemma she couldn't get to grips with yet but, whatever happened now, she knew that she never need look back again, shackled by the chains of grief. Then she shook her head as complete exhaustion came over her.

'Thanks for the offer, Andy, but I'd better drive myself back—I'll need the car in a few hours for work!'

'You know, darling, I don't want to pry, but you haven't seemed yourself lately—even after all that lovely sun on the beach yesterday afternoon, you look so pale. Is anything wrong at work?'

Lily's face puckered anxiously across at Rosie as they ate their evening meal together. 'I think you've been overdoing it, you know, with this partner off with his back and everything.'

Rosie coloured slightly and concentrated rather hard on cutting Amy's toast into small squares.

'Not at all!' she said lightly. 'Actually, Roddy's coming back on Monday. He's made a very good recovery, so the load will be much lighter.'

Lily looked at her sharply. 'Oh, dear—does that mean that Andy will be leaving? He's only a locum, isn't he? But he's such a nice man! You'd miss him, wouldn't you?'

'He won't be leaving yet,' replied Rosie lightly. 'He's been so invaluable that we're going to try and keep him on—if he'll stay. Now it's the holiday season, we're bound to get even busier, with tourists. It's amazing how many of them are ill and have accidents when they're here—last night was an awful example.'

'That must have drained you,' said Lily sympathetically. 'You should have an early night tonight. Let me put Amy to bed, you sit on the terrace and relax and then I'll come down and we'll discuss where you could go for a holiday. It's obvious to me you need a break!'

There was no doubt about it, thought Rosie, sipping a long drink thoughtfully as she sat out on the little terrace, she would have to tell Lily very soon that she was having a baby. It wasn't fair to keep her in the dark. She drew a deep breath of the balmy evening air and reflected how much of a rock Lily had been to her since she'd been on her own. Despite her smoky, joky manner, she was a very wise woman, rarely shocked or judgmental at any worries Rosie might confide to her. This news, however, might shake her more than usual!

Lily came out with her usual small tot of brandy—'only medicinal', as she liked to say. She sat beside Rosie. 'Amy's out like a light, the little sweetheart,' she said. Then she lit a cigarette, and turned towards Rosie, a steely light in her bright eyes.

'Now, my dear,' she said firmly. 'I don't believe a word of your protestations that nothing's wrong. I've known you too long not to realise that you have something on your mind—and I jolly well want to know what it is!'

Rosie tilted her head back against her seat and looked up at the cerulean sky, just beginning to be touched with pink as the sun started to dip. She couldn't hide her secret from Lily for ever.

'I don't know how to tell you this—and you're never going to believe it,' she said slowly. 'But the fact is, Lily, I'm pregnant!'

There was a stunned silence. Lily took a deep inhalation of her cigarette, and then a large swig of her brandy. '*What* did you say?' she said at last. 'Am I hearing right?'

Rosie nodded. 'You heard right,' she said. Then she burst into tears.

Immediately Lily sprang up and knelt down beside her, putting her arms round Rosie's shoulders.

'Darling, please, don't cry. I didn't mean to upset you and sound shocked—you just took me rather by surprise!'

'You'll think I'm completely mad.'

Lily shook her head and stroked Rosie's hand. 'Just give me a minute to get used to the idea! You know, I love you whatever happens, and actually the thought of a new baby is really wonderful. It will be lovely for Amy to have a little brother or sister.' She gave Rosie a sparkling smile. 'And what does the father think of this?'

'He...he doesn't know,' muttered Rosie hollowly. 'I just don't know how I can tell him—or even *if* I should tell him.'

'I don't understand...' Lily went back to her chair and sat down, staring at Rosie in a perplexed way. 'Why should you not be able to tell him?'

'Because—oh, because he's got commitments elsewhere. He may even move abroad—and that's something I could never do!'

'But, my dear girl, he has to know—he has a right to know. He might have "commitments", as you put it, but now he's got another commitment. He'll just have to sort it out with you.'

'You don't know who it is,' said Rosie wretchedly.

Lily looked at her scornfully. 'I can make a pretty good guess.' She laughed at Rosie's surprised face and stubbed out her cigarette. 'You don't have to be a genius to know that Andy Templeton's madly in love with you—and I'm pretty sure,' she added shrewdly, 'that you're not averse to his company either!'

Rosie reddened. 'Is it so obvious that I...I love him?'

'You'd be mad not to! He's absolutely gorgeous!'

She looked at Rosie mischievously. 'And how long did it take for you two to get together?'

Rosie pulled a strand of hair back from her forehead, a blush of embarrassment rising to her face. 'Not very long, actually—about seven hours from when I first met him!'

Lily nodded sagely. 'The weekend conference! I had a feeling that more happened there than discussions on local health!' She leant back in her chair. 'You know, Rosie, I think you do Andy a disservice to think he wouldn't want to know about this baby. I'm sure he's a man who would face up to his responsibilities—and I think he would be thrilled to think you were having a baby together!'

'But he'll think I'm trying to trap him. I don't think he would want a permanent relationship!'

Lily raised her eyes to heaven. 'I've never heard such nonsense. What makes you so sure about that? And anyway, he might just be delighted that there's something that's going to bind you together.'

'It could ruin his future plans...'

'Rosie Loveday—you know that every child deserves two loving parents.'

'That's just what Andy said,' murmured Rosie.

'Well, then, think about it. Poor little Amy didn't have a choice when Tony died before she was even born. How unfair it would be to deprive this little one of a father, just because you seem to be frightened of telling the man!' She looked fiercely at Rosie. 'You've got to tell him—it would be grossly unfair to you both if you didn't.'

Rosie gazed silently at her hands, twisting nervously in her lap. Of course Lily was right—how could she deprive Andy of the knowledge of this child, or the child of its own father?

She stood up and looked down at Lily with a rueful smile, then kissed her quickly. 'You're right, Lily—I'm a fool not to have seen it before. I knew you'd know the way to go, you wise old thing! I'll tell him as soon as possible—perhaps after work tomorrow.' She gave a little giggle. 'You know, I can't wait to see his face!'

Lily leant forward in her chair and looked at her seriously. 'Just tell me one thing, darling—how do you feel about this baby? Are you thrilled or sorry about it?'

Rosie hugged her arms around herself and laughed. 'I can't remember feeling so excited for a long time. If Andy takes to the idea, it'll make everything perfect!'

It seemed a summer of beautiful days, thought Rosie, swinging her car happily into the health centre's car park. The day matched her mood, sunny and sparkling. Somehow she didn't feel nervous now about telling Andy of his impending fatherhood. Everything she'd been worried about seemed to have been resolved after her talk with Lily. She couldn't wait for the end of the afternoon.

Ben was riffling through his correspondence in the office behind Reception. He looked up over his glasses at Rosie as she came swinging in.

'Ah, Rosie! I'm afraid we're going to have to fit in a few extra today…we're rather short-handed.'

Rosie looked at him questioningly. 'What's happened?'

'Good job we've got Roddy starting back on

Monday. Andy's had to abandon things here rather swiftly—he took a flight to Chicago last night.'

'What?' Rosie's mouth went dry and her voice cracked slightly. 'Why—what's happened?'

Ben spread his hands out helplessly. 'His ex-wife's new husband has been seriously injured in an industrial accident and she's involved in looking after him. Andy's gone to help her and look after his son. I don't know what his long-term plans are, but he'll probably be some time sorting things out. I suppose he'll end up doing whatever's best for Keiron.'

'You mean…he could end up staying in the States?'

Ben shrugged. 'It's a possibility. Keiron's probably happily settled at his school with his own friends. Andy may feel it would be cruel to move him. Well, Andy was only a stopgap after all. It would have been a bonus to have him stay on as he's an excellent doctor and the patients love him, but we'll just have to manage without him!'

'Just have to manage without him…' The words hammered in Rosie's head, echoing and reverberating cruelly as she walked unseeingly to her room. She sat down at her desk and switched on her computer, watching as it booted up. Of course she'd manage, she thought numbly. She'd done so before, hadn't she? Made a life for herself when Tony had died? Now she'd have to face up to the fact that Andy would probably never come back to England, and that, however fond he was of her, when Keiron needed him he dropped everything!

For the first time she noticed an envelope on her desk addressed to her in scrawled handwriting. She tore it open.

'My dear Rosie,' she read. 'I'm so sorry I've had to

go so suddenly to Chicago without saying goodbye. Ben has probably told you that Sonia's husband has been badly injured and she can't look after Keiron by herself. I don't know how long I'll be over there, but I hope things will be clearer soon. Take care of yourself. Love to you, Amy and Lily—Andy.'

Rosie folded the letter neatly and put it back in the envelope. There was no doubt about it. Andy Templeton was history. From now on it was just Amy and herself—and the new baby.

CHAPTER TEN

ANDY TEMPLETON looked at his son patiently. 'Film or fishing, Keiron?'

The young boy's eyes lit up. 'Can we go fishing, Dad—by the little bay on the lake? It reminds me of the house in England and the little cove there. It's really neat!'

Andy grinned wryly. 'You like the little cove?'

'Sure—and the house, too, with all those secret passages!'

'Perhaps we'll go back and see them, then, when we've helped your mum sort things out here.'

Keiron nodded seriously. 'Yeah, cool—I'd like that.'

Father and son were sitting on the verandah of the beautiful whiteboard house that belonged to Sonia and Roger. The large garden was filled with the paraphernalia of a young boy's activities—a football, a baseball bat, a basketball ring on the wall and a blue scooter carelessly flung on the ground. Keiron got up and started to kick the football against the wall, then he looked across at his father and frowned.

'Is Roger going to die? He's pretty sick, isn't he?'

Andy walked over to his son and put his arm round the boy's shoulders. 'I don't think he'll die, Keiron, but he may never be in the best of health. They think he's injured his back very badly, which might stop him walking.'

Keiron stopped kicking the ball and leant against the wall, watching his father carefully. 'Suppose he did die,' he persisted. 'Then perhaps you and Mom might get together again, huh?'

There was a heart-breaking wistfulness in his son's voice that caught at Andy's heart. He sighed. It was hard for Keiron to believe that he and Sonia would never get together again.

'You know Mum and I are good friends, and we both love you very much,' he said gently. 'But I'm afraid we aren't very good at living together—we're happier apart.'

Keiron made a face and kicked a stone on the driveway as they walked to the car. 'I'd like to be part of a proper family,' he muttered. 'Most of the guys at school have families, brothers and sisters. I'm the only one who's got no one. And now Mom's got no time for me 'cos she's so busy looking after Roger...'

Andy ruffled the boy's hair affectionately. 'Now you're feeling sorry for yourself! You've got a lot of people who love you—and loads of friends. And aren't I here to look after you while Mum's busy? Count your blessings, my boy! And now let's get fishing—the rods are in the car already!'

As they drove off to the lake, Andy glanced at his son's grave profile. He was a wonderful little boy, and he'd always seemed to accept what his parents told him quite calmly, yet underneath that apparently acquiescent façade was a sensitive child who wanted nothing more than to be part of an ordinary family. One thing was for sure. Keiron had pinpointed a very important fact—Sonia would be totally occupied from now on with a husband who would be confined to a wheelchair for the rest of his life.

Andy gazed at the straight road ahead, his knuckles white as his hands gripped the steering-wheel. He had to think of the future—his future as much as Keiron's. Once he got a job in the States, he couldn't see himself returning to England for some time—and the paradox was, he thought bitterly, that he had never wanted to be home so much in his life. He loved Keiron with all his heart, but his life wouldn't be complete unless he was with Rosie—and what kind of a future would she have with him? He guessed she wouldn't want to leave Lily and come and live in America, and he saw no prospect of going back for a long time. No, it was best that he didn't let her know how much he needed and longed for her. It would be fairer to Rosie, and Amy, if he allowed her to get on with her own life without him.

The rain lashed down so hard against the windows in Ben's room that it was like being in an aquarium, thought Rosie gloomily, staring out at the rivulets of water that poured from the gutters. The weather reflected her mood. She still couldn't get her head around the fact that just as she'd determined to tell Andy about her baby, he'd vanished back to America. It was a cold and empty feeling—but in a way she was relieved she hadn't burdened him with the truth before. Whatever happened, Keiron would always come first with Andy.

She reflected on the e-mail she'd received from Andy. It had been a brief acknowledgement of her letter to him, saying how sorry she'd been to hear about the accident to Keiron's stepfather. She could visualise the e-mail vividly—it had been fairly formal and, considering their former relationship, distant and cold.

Dear Rosie, Thank you for your kind letter regarding Roger. Although he's been seriously injured, life is starting to settle down into a routine here. I'm going to take some qualifying exams so that I can hopefully get some work in Chicago. It's a wonderful city with plenty to do, and Keiron and I are enjoying ourselves immensely. Hope life is fine for you and Amy. Best wishes, Andy.

If that wasn't a clear indication that Andy intended to cut his life off from her for ever, she didn't know what was, she thought sadly. No mention of meeting again, or of when he might come back to England. How ironic it was that just when she knew with all her heart and soul that she loved him with every fibre of her being, he should disappear out of her life for ever.

The murmur of her partners' voices in the background brought her back to the present. They were discussing the practice's drug strategy and the various new drugs that had been introduced in the market.

'I've been reading about a new drug that's currently being tested on treating *Helcobactor pylori* infections,' Ben was saying. 'They're running trials now—it sounds promising.' He pushed a journal towards Roddy. 'This is the paper on it—I think you'll find it interesting if you could read it some time. They may market it next year.'

Next year, thought Rosie numbly, I shall have my new baby. And, like a rerun of an old film, there won't be any father to welcome it. She felt the hollowness of despair, just as she had when Tony had died, as if her future had been whipped away from her. She bit her lip and flicked a look at the two men on either side of her. They would have to know about her baby sooner or later, but she would never tell them that Andy was the father. Andy had another life in another land now, and she and he had different paths to follow.

'I think that's all for now,' said Ben, gathering up some papers from the desk. The discussion had come to an end, and they got up to go.

'Glad you both got on with Andy Templeton,' remarked Roddy as they walked out. 'He's a good man. Lucky he was able to come when I had my accident, wasn't it?'

'It certainly was,' agreed Ben enthusiastically. Rosie nodded silently, an empty feeling in the pit of her stomach.

'I just wonder what he'll do now. I believe that Roger, his wife's new husband, will be wheelchair-bound, poor chap. It's early days, of course, but it seems he's paralysed below the chest, although that could improve over the next few weeks.'

Rosie looked in horror at Roddy. 'That's tragic,' she said, appalled at the news being even worse than she'd thought. 'How terrible for them all. I suppose Andy will stay out there, then?'

Roddy shrugged helplessly. 'I don't know at all. He just e-mailed me with the news about Roger, but didn't reveal his future plans. Probably doesn't even know what he's going to do himself.'

Ben shook his head. 'I can't see Andy ever coming back here. His future's got to be with his son.'

Each doctor went to their own room and Rosie sat down blindly at her desk. Two tears rolled down her cheeks and she brushed them away impatiently. 'And *my* future's with my daughter and new baby,' she muttered fiercely to herself. She punched the button to signal on the display board in the waiting room that she was ready for the first patient and fixed a bright smile on her face.

The low autumn sun cast long shadows of their figures over the field as Rosie and Amy and the dog walked over the field at the back of the cottage. The Indian summer they'd been enjoying was coming to an end. There was a chill in the air and the earthy smell of newly ploughed land.

'Boggle! Boggle! Come back here! We must go in now!'

Rosie shielded her eyes from the sun and watched the dog bounding back to her and Amy across the fields, his ears flapping wildly, a huge stick protruding out of his mouth. He flung it down on the ground in front of them and looked up hopefully from one to the other.

Rosie laughed. 'Sorry, old boy. We're not throwing it any more, are we, Amy? It's time for tea and it's getting cold.' She pulled a lead from her pocket and fastened it to the dog's collar, then bent down and adjusted Amy's anorak, pulling the fur-lined hood over the little girl's head. 'Come on, my darling, let's go back to Lily.'

Amy picked up the stick Boggle had dropped and began to skip ahead on sturdy little legs. 'Come on, Mummy!' she shouted. 'You skip, too!'

A few more weeks and it wouldn't be so easy to skip, thought Rosie, panting slightly beside her daughter. Being five months pregnant, she had begun to fill out and had decided that next week she would definitely have to tell Ben Cummings and Roddy Turner that for a few months early in the next year she wouldn't be available—before they guessed! She had been putting it off for weeks, loth to see the questioning look in their eyes when she told them her news.

She slowed down to a brisk walk and smiled at Amy, now holding Boggle's lead and being pulled along the path by him. Life wasn't too bad. She was healthy, she loved her job and she had people round her whom she loved. Only sometimes…a lot of times…she longed for Andy, longed to share with him the hopes and dreams she had for this new baby. After many weeks he had written to her again, explaining that Roger, although regaining some use of his legs, was still very frail and needed full-time assistance. He hadn't mentioned the future, this time sending only his 'best wishes'. She had found his cold attitude inexplicable and hurtful, but it had confirmed her in her belief that she was right not tell him that he was the father of her baby.

She watched a flock of rooks flying across the reddening sky. The days were getting shorter, and any day now the clocks would go back and winter would have begun. She picked Amy up as the little girl began to flag, and hugged her close, burying her head in the warm silkiness of her round little cheek. Amy giggled and wound her arms round Rosie's neck.

'I want cakes for tea,' she confided to her mother. 'And biscuits—lots and lots!'

Rosie laughed. With Amy around, how could she be sad for long?

They went through the gate at the back garden of the cottage and in through the back door. Rosie pulled off Amy's boots, then with more difficulty managed to pull her own wellies off. Lily had been making scones and the lovely warm smell of them pervaded the kitchen. She couldn't resist pinching one from the tray where they lay temptingly on top of the stove. Taking a large bite from it, she walked into the lounge.

She stopped suddenly. Someone was standing looking out of the window with his back to the door, a tall, broad figure. With the light in her eyes Rosie found it difficult to focus at first, then the man turned round, and for a confused moment Rosie wondered if she was hallucinating. Clear blue eyes stared into hers for a long, long minute, an unreadable expression in their depths. Then a familiar deep voice said very quietly, 'Rosie Loveday—why the hell didn't you tell me what's been happening?'

Suddenly Rosie felt her knees buckle and sat down on the settee. 'Andy…' she managed. 'Andy…what are you doing here? I thought you were in America. No one said you'd come back!'

'Never mind all that.' His voice was harsh. 'I want to know why you kept me in the dark about your baby…*our* baby!' He looked across at her grimly, a muscle working in his cheek. 'Was it going to be kept a secret for ever—was I never going to know that I'd fathered a child?'

Rosie looked up at him wordlessly, her heart hammering against her ribs in the astonishment of seeing him. Her eyes drank in every aspect of him greedily—his strapping figure, strong mobile face and full lips. He hadn't changed. He was just as she had dreamed about him every night since he'd left. And now he was *here*—here in this room, a few yards away from her!

'I…I thought you had too many worries to load you with mine,' she said at last, trying to sort out the myriad thoughts that whirled round in her mind.

Andy strode across the room and squatted down beside her, looking intensely into her eyes. 'How ridiculous can you get? For God's sake, Rosie, it wasn't just your worry. Two people made this baby and one of them was me!' His voice softened and he took her hands in his. 'Did you think so little of me that you thought I couldn't handle this—take on the responsibility? Surely you know me better than that!'

Rosie stood up abruptly and walked away from him, then turned round, her expression defensive. 'It wasn't that easy. You'd made it pretty clear that Keiron would always be your priority—and you were right to make him so. When you went back to America it seemed to make the whole situation more complicated...'

He snorted derisively. 'Surely you could have written and told me! Why did you want to keep this to yourself? You have one child who has no father—why inflict that on another one? Don't you think that's rather selfish?'

An angry flush spread over Rosie's cheeks, and her voice became more harsh. 'Don't you dare tell me I'm selfish,' she said tersely. 'As a matter of fact, I was going to tell you about the baby before you disappeared to America—although you'd made it pretty clear to me before that you didn't want any more children, that Keiron was more than enough to handle!'

'You certainly seem to have made some odd assumptions,' he said sardonically. 'It seems every little remark I made was taken very seriously!'

Rosie looked at him challengingly. 'You certainly didn't give me the impression you were in a hurry to come back. To be honest, the e-mails you sent implied that your life here was over. You barely enquired about me or Amy.'

He bit his lip. 'I'm well aware that I must have sounded a little cold...'

Rosie gave a scornful laugh. 'You sounded as if you were writing to a distant acquaintance!'

He took her hands in his and looked at her with serious eyes. 'I did that on purpose, Rosie, sweetheart. I didn't want you to feel…attached in any way to me—not with my problems.'

Rosie shrugged. 'So you've come back. Would you have done so anyway, or is it only because you've heard I'm having your baby?'

'Not only that,' he said gently. 'For God's sake, you don't know how much I've longed to see you, Rosie.' He began to pace the floor restlessly. 'Surely you can't deny that we had something more than attraction between us. Didn't we set each other alight?'

Rosie's face coloured as he held her gaze for a second, then he continued, 'When I had to go to the States, I felt the future I could offer you was something you wouldn't want—to live in America, away from your loved ones, your new job, your lovely little cottage… Why should I uproot you, and make you take on all my baggage? It would have been selfish, to say the least. That's why I didn't want you to feel we were…involved.'

She stared at him coolly, although she felt her heart racing. 'And has the situation changed?'

'My feelings for you have never changed,' Andy replied. 'But other things have—I'll tell you about those in a minute. But now we're having a baby it doesn't matter what the situation is, surely. Our duty is to give the child a happy home, two loving parents—don't you agree with that?'

Rosie felt a surge of compassion for the man standing in front of her. He was good and kind, wanting to do the best for those he loved. And he was right—their baby deserved the best of everything. She loved Andy so much, and had done from the day she'd met him. She knew that now, and the fact she had never been sure that he would be fully committed to her didn't matter any more.

She brushed a tendril of hair away from her face nervously. 'I really did mean to tell you. It...it just seemed you had another life over there that I could never be part of. It didn't seem fair to burden you—'

Andy jumped up in exasperation. 'Burden me, my foot! Rosie Loveday—I don't know how many children we'll end up having but, by God, I want to know about each and every one!'

There was a short silence, then Rosie whispered, 'What did you just say?'

Suddenly his fierce demeanour relaxed and a wide grin split his face. 'I said I didn't know how many children we'd have—probably one at a time!'

'What...what do you mean...?' Her voice shook, her brown eyes wide.

His arms slid round her waist and he pulled her towards him until their bodies touched. 'It means, you silly woman, that we're going to be together for ever and ever. I've not come back merely to be on the sidelines! We're going to be a proper family—you, me, Amy and Keiron. And, of course, junior here.' He patted her stomach gently. 'Perhaps we ought to set the date for the wedding very soon, don't you think?'

Somewhere inside her, little waves of happiness started to ripple through her body. This was unreal, wonderful and totally bewildering! She shook her head as if to clear her thoughts. 'I don't understand all this... How did you find out about the baby? Does everyone know?'

He chuckled. 'Your Aunt Lily is a very wise woman,' he commented. 'I think she reckoned that I ought to be made aware that I was to become a father, and if you didn't tell me—then she would! I received a very informative letter at the end of last week. I came back on the first flight available!'

'But what about Keiron—and your ex-wife? How can she look after your son?'

His eyes danced. 'Things have a way of working out. Of course, Roger is English and basically wanted to come back to his home here to recuperate. He was setting up a business in Chicago and only planned to stay there two or three years anyway.'

'At least Sonia's looking after him.'

Andy gave a wry smile. 'Perhaps I'm being cynical, but I feel the prospect of being a member of the aristocracy and living in a splendid castle seems to have helped Sonia overcome her homesickness! So you see, my sweet, there really is no reason why we can't all live over here!'

'So Keiron would have both his parents in England?'

'That's right. He would spend most of his time with us because Sonia feels Roger is now too old and frail to have a young child around all the time, but I think Keiron loves the thought that at least we're all in the same country!'

Her eyes were bright with wonder. 'It…it just doesn't seem possible. You're here, and you're going to stay!'

'Got it in one!' He turned her face towards his and kissed her gently with soft lips. 'I think I should tell you,' he whispered in her ear, 'that as soon as you came in, Lily took Amy out to tea with a friend. She wanted us to have an hour or two to get to know each other again!'

Rosie stared at him, then started to laugh helplessly. 'Andy Templeton—you schemer! I just can't believe all this is happening!'

The little waves of happiness became great rollers washing over her, and with all the naturalness in the world, she wound her arms round Andy's neck and pressed her lips to his. He held her back from him for a moment, and looked down at her with such tenderness and love that her stomach gave that old familiar somersault of longing and delight.

'My sweet darling,' he whispered, 'what have you been through, trying to deal with this on your own? I want you to promise me—never, never keep anything from me again!'

Then he bent his mouth to hers and kissed her with passion, his tongue teasing her lips apart, his hands exploring her body. Rosie felt her insides liquefy with a desire she'd dreamed of so often in the last months, and with abandon she pulled him down on the rug beside the fire.

She looked at him with an impish grin. 'That's a pretty tall order.' She grinned. 'You'll have to convince me of that!'

He looked down at her, laughter in the depths of his eyes. 'I'll do my best,' he promised.

Their eyes locked for a second, then with mutual delight and unspoken consent they started to undress each other, the long months of waiting feeding their desire. Andy slowly peeled off her jumper and bent to kiss the soft skin of her breasts and stomach, before helping her to wriggle out of her jeans. Then, with studied concentration, Rosie undid his shirt and trousers, marvelling at his hard, muscular body, the strength of his arousal. They knelt in front of each other for a moment, their naked bodies barely touching, and his blue gaze feasted on her rounded curves before his hands moved over her breasts and back, pulling her towards him, his fingers skilfully exploring the most intimate places of her body until she moaned with pleasure.

'Beautiful Rosie,' he said huskily, his lips trailing fire down her body. 'It's been so long… Do you know how much I love you, how often I've dreamed of doing this again with you?'

Rosie gave a low laugh. 'This time,' she whispered, 'you don't have to ask me if I really want you to make love to me—I think you know!'

Then all time stood still as their bodies became one in a glorious, passionate reunion.

'Hey, Amy! Don't drop all the cutlery on the floor! We're trying to lay the table, not clear it! Why don't you bring in that cake you made with Lily?'

Keiron grinned after Amy's little figure as she bustled out to do as he said. She was some little kid, he thought affectionately. She followed him around like a puppy. It was rather nice to be adored and needed by the little girl—and he enjoyed spending time with her. He glanced round the room. He liked it here. It was so cosy and he was beginning to get used to being part of a family unit—America seemed a long long time ago.

Amy trotted back with a plate of well-cooked buns held precariously in her hands, followed by Lily bearing a trayful of delicious-looking sandwiches.

'Here we are, Keiron—put that in the centre of the table. They'll be here any minute…'

Lily looked flushed and excited, nervous energy having enabled her to clean the cottage from top to bottom that morning. She went to the window and peered out, then gave a little squeal.

'Quick, my darlings! They're driving up now!'

The three of them ran to the door and flung it open. Andy was helping Rosie out of the car. He turned round and smiled at them all, his smile widening as he saw the banner Keiron had placed over the lintel. WELCOME TO OUR NEW BABY, it said in big red letters. An amazing array of squiggles and crosses surrounded the words—those had been Amy's contribution.

Rosie walked up the path, her arms filled with a pink-faced bundle wrapped in a white shawl.

She bent down towards them and pulled the shawl away from the baby's face.

'Keiron, Amy,' she said softly, 'your new little sister's dying to meet you. Come and say hello to Carla!'

They crowded round and looked at the tiny baby with awe. Keiron put out a gentle hand and stroked her cheek. 'She sure is pretty,' he said softly. He looked up at Rosie and grinned. 'Now I've got two sisters, haven't I?' He looked across at his father. 'Next time, can we have a boy?'

Andy smiled, a very tender smile, at them all. 'Now, that will be another chapter,' he murmured.

Modern Romance™
...seduction and
passion guaranteed

Tender Romance™
...love affairs that
last a lifetime

Medical Romance™
...medical drama on
the pulse

Historical Romance™
...rich, vivid and
passionate

Sensual Romance™
...sassy, sexy and seductive

27 new titles every month.

*With all kinds of Romance for
every kind of mood...*

MILLS & BOON®

Makes any time special™

MAT4RS

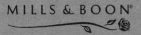

MILLS & BOON®

Medical Romance™

THE DOCTORS' BABY by *Marion Lennox*

Part 4 of Parents Wanted

As Bay Beach's only doctor, Emily Mainwaring is too busy for distractions. Unfortunately, there are two large ones headed her way! The first is an orphaned baby boy, whom Emily longs to adopt. The second is Jonas Lunn, a gorgeous surgeon from Sydney. Jonas is more than interested in a passionate affair – but what Emily needs from him is marriage...

LIFE SUPPORT by *Jennifer Taylor*

For Senior Registrar Michelle Roberts, the daily crises of St Justin's emergency department provided all the drama she needed. It took Dominic Walsh to help confront her own hurt and motivation, and suddenly, persuading Michelle to accept all the love and support she'd been missing became Dominic's number one priority.

RIVALS IN PRACTICE by *Alison Roberts*

When a storm throws a rural New Zealand town into chaos, Dr Jennifer Tremaine's professional prowess is put under pressure. Then, surgeon Andrew Stephenson steps into the fray. She and Drew haven't seen each other since medical school, and now things are very different. Beneath the old rivalry stirs a new sensation...

On sale 3rd May 2002

Available at most branches of WH Smith, Tesco, Martins, Borders, Eason, Sainsbury's and most good paperback bookshops. 0402/03a

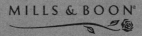

MILLS & BOON

Medical Romance™

EMERGENCY RESCUE by *Abigail Gordon*

Dr Jemima Penrose's return home is difficult enough without developing a relationship with new colleague Jack Trelawney. Jack is a lifeboat volunteer, and Jemima is all too aware of the danger that places him in. However, when faced with the possibility of losing Jack, Jemima realises he's worth risking her heart for…

THE CONSULTANT'S RECOVERY
by *Gill Sanderson*

When a freak accident left Jonathan Knight blinded, the charismatic consultant was determined to take control of his life. And that was where Tania Richardson came in. As she taught him to cope Jonathan found himself drawn to her. But Tania was holding back, and somehow it was all linked to his chances of recovery…

THE PREGNANT INTERN by *Carol Marinelli*

Surgeon Jeremy Foster is a carefree bachelor. Until he meets his new intern! Dr Alice Masters – six months pregnant – brings out instincts he hadn't known he possessed. Jeremy worries about her working too hard and he hates the thought of her bringing up a baby alone. But there isn't much he can do - unless he swaps the role of boss for that of husband!

On sale 3rd May 2002

Available at most branches of WH Smith, Tesco, Martins, Borders, Eason, Sainsbury's and most good paperback bookshops.

0402/03b

Coming in July

The Ultimate
Betty Neels
Collection

* A stunning 12 book collection beautifully packaged for you to collect each month from bestselling author Betty Neels.

* Loved by millions of women around the world, this collection of heartwarming stories will be a joy to treasure forever.

2 FREE

books and a surprise gift!

We would like to take this opportunity to thank you for reading this Mills & Boon® book by offering you the chance to take TWO more specially selected titles from the Medical Romance™ series absolutely FREE! We're also making this offer to introduce you to the benefits of the Reader Service™—

★ FREE home delivery
★ FREE gifts and competitions
★ FREE monthly Newsletter
★ Exclusive Reader Service discount
★ Books available before they're in the shops

Accepting these FREE books and gift places you under no obligation to buy, you may cancel at any time, even after receiving your free shipment. Simply complete your details below and return the entire page to the address below. *You don't even need a stamp!*

YES! Please send me 2 free Medical Romance books and a surprise gift. I understand that unless you hear from me, I will receive 4 superb new titles every month for just £2.55 each, postage and packing free. I am under no obligation to purchase any books and may cancel my subscription at any time. The free books and gift will be mine to keep in any case.

M2ZEA

Ms/Mrs/Miss/Mr ....Initials.................................
                                                BLOCK CAPITALS PLEASE
Surname ....
Address ....

....
....Postcode.................................

Send this whole page to:
UK: FREEPOST CN81, Croydon, CR9 3WZ
EIRE: PO Box 4546, Kilcock, County Kildare (stamp required)